\ _ь ME

THE LAST VOCARI: BOOK 1

ELENA LAWSON

THORN HOUSE
PUBLISHING

The vampire's final breath left his pale lips like a sigh.

I toed his corpse with the tip of my heeled boot just to make sure. *Yep, he's dead alright.*

Deader than dead, really, since he could have been changed years ago. It takes a while, but their hearts *do* stop beating. That bit was true.

Strange then, how ramming a metal stake through the soft tissue and muscle killed them. I mean, if it wasn't beating anyway...

I shook my head—I'd never really cared how it all worked, just that it did. I knelt down on the asphalt, careful not to kneel in the rapidly growing ring of deep red around his broken body and used his denim jacket to wipe off my stakes before sheathing them back into the leather rings on my inner thighs beneath my leather skirt.

Leaning in, I peeled back his eyelids.

"*Damn*," I whispered, pushing the pale flaps of skin back down to cover his unseeing green eyes. He wasn't the one I hunted. But he had fangs and the reek of fresh blood on his breath and that was evidence enough against him in my books.

Rising, I stretched out my back and cracked my neck. Sighed. I searched the deserted area around back of the bowling alley. It was a Tuesday night—well past midnight. I didn't like leaving the bodies out in the open like this, but I didn't see I had much other choice this time. This one had been a bonus. I wasn't out to hunt—with my truck, tarp, shovel and rope. I'd been doing my laundry at the 24hr joint down the strip and left for some air and a cup of coffee when I saw him.

The bloodsucker looked like he'd just come from a feeding. With color in his cheeks and the metallic reek of blood on him. I only hoped he'd left his victim alive, otherwise the police would be dealing with two bodies in the morgue tomorrow. Notifying one family that their sister, aunt, friend or father wouldn't be coming home ever again.

I shuddered.

Ah! A dumpster. The green metal bin crouched against the weathered brick of the building, a few paces from a door marked 'employees only', but a staggering

2

twenty feet or so from where I stood with the decaying vampire at my feet.

"Hope you're not as heavy as you look," I said to him, and hoisted his body onto my shoulder, grunting with the effort. His blood dripped down my shoulder, staining my shirt.

"You owe me a shirt," I said, exasperated.

His limp corpse proved heavier than I anticipated. But nothing I couldn't manage. I'd conditioned my body for this. How else could a human woman take out fully matured vampires? Practice.

And patience.

And a little something *extra.*

They were the only reasons I was still alive and so many of them were dead. I lifted the lid of the green bin and shoved him inside, a horrid smell wafting up from the black bags beneath him the moment he hit them. *Ugh.* I reached into his pocket and fished out his wallet, glad to see there were more than few hundreds tucked inside the flaps.

Score.

Reaching into the knot of black hair at the back of my head, I tugged free the small rosebud I'd tucked there before leaving the motel and tossed it atop the vamp's chest. The lid fell closed and I stepped back, holding my breath to ward off the stench.

I felt sorry for the poor employee who found him. It looked like rain tonight, but tomorrow would be hot as hell if the weatherman was to be trusted. And there's nothing worse than the smell of dead guy in the morning.

Here was hoping the little old lady back at the Soap 'n Suds had finished her washing for the night. With this much blood on me, I'd wind up giving her a heart attack otherwise.

"Seth!" Someone called from down the street, cursing under his breath. I'd always had great hearing, so when I heard the unmistakable sound of a numbers being dialed on a cell, I flipped open the wallet in my hand.

There, in the little plastic covered card-slot was an i.d. card. Either a very good fake, or this guy was more recently changed. He looked just like in the photo. Seth Carfax.

I rolled my eyes at the darkened sky. *Couldn't I have just one day off?*

Any second now the other vamp would smell the blood of his friend and be around the building.

Looks like laundry will have to wait.

But I couldn't risk getting any more blood on my clothes. If anyone spotted me on my way back to the laundry, I would draw too much attention. I didn't feel like dealing with the local authorities tonight.

The soles of the new player's shoes slapped the pavement in quick steps as he came around the edge of the building. I was already on the ground, feigning injury. Just a pretty girl, helpless and all alone in the dark. No one around to hear me scream.

Worked almost every time.

He froze mid-dialing, and I resisted the urge to loose a sigh of relief. I hadn't checked the one in the dumpster's pockets for a phone, but I knew a ringing dumpster would be pretty fucking suspicious if he completed that call.

His lips parted as he took in the sight of me. Dressed in a low-cut halter and short leather skirt. My boots hugging my calves all the way to my knees.

"Please," I said, in my most pleading high-pitched voice. "Please help me."

The vampire drew nearer, and I saw that I hadn't been wrong about what he was. They had an air about them. I *felt* the presence of them in the atmosphere when they were near. Another learned ability.

He walked over to me, and I hoped he wouldn't see the enormous streak of blood twenty feet away. That he wouldn't follow the drips to the trash bin over by the wall.

But no, his focus narrowed squarely on me.

That's it. Come and get me.

The vampire stood tall and lanky. Maybe six feet. Broad through the shoulders with a trim waist. A shock of white-blonde hair offset his dark eyes and sharp cheekbones. He reminded me of someone I used to know. Too bad he wasn't still human—I'd climb him like a tree if he were. Such a waste.

"I can't get up," I said as he approached, doing my best to hold his attention. "My leg, its—"

He leaned down and I got him. His eyes locked on mine—giving me the only leverage I needed.

"Don't move."

He stilled.

I focused my mind on him and only him. It was the only way it worked, and even then, it could falter.

He opened his mouth to speak as I rose to my feet. "Quiet," I commanded.

His lips sealed closed. A crease formed between his brows. His lips curled in distaste. They really didn't like it when I used their own ability against them. Compulsion was *their* power. On top of speed, agility, heightened senses and immortality.

But it was also *mine*.

"You're wondering what I am, aren't you?" I asked, my voice teasing as sweat beaded on both my brow and his. The focus of keeping him bent to my will exerted me more than any street fight could. My pulse soared and my chest tightened, constricting my breath to small, sharp inhales. I'd learned to get used to it, though. I could hold him like this for nearly an hour if I tried hard enough.

I shrugged when he didn't answer, smiling to myself knowing that he couldn't even if he wanted to.

"I'm lucky, I guess."

It was all I would allow myself to think. The fact I shared this trait with my victims made my skin itch. I hated it, but it was necessary. And very likely the only reason I hadn't been drained dry yet. And the only reason I got away with doing everything I did.

"But you," I said, circling him. "Aren't so lucky tonight."

I pulled out one of my metal stakes from between my legs and twirled it in my fingers, making sure he caught the glint of the cold hard steel in the moonlight. He made a strained sound in his throat, and I crouched down in front of him, meeting his eyes again, disappointed to find that they were both a dull brown. Not the guy, either.

"What was that? Speak up."

He took a short, gasping breath, his eyes wide as he sputtered. "The Black Rose."

Huh?

"I know who you are," he said in a rush and my blood chilled. "They're coming for you. They'll kill—"

"That's enough," I ordered. I was losing my edge. The compulsion slipping as his words wreaked havoc on my nerves. Stupid of me to allow him to speak at all. It didn't happen often, given that only the strongest and oldest of them could compel at all...but if they compelled me before I could compel them...

Well, let's just say I didn't ever want to know what would become of me if that happened.

"Time to meet your maker," I said, my tone bored as I reeled back and plunged the sharp edged metal into his hunched back, throwing all my body weight into the swing to make sure I broke through the bones of his ribs and hit my target.

His breath left him in a great *whoosh.* He choked a bit on the inhale, and then he fell. My compulsion releasing him at the same moment his unnatural life ended.

The Black Rose.

I wiped off my stake on the ass of his jeans.

So, they had a name for me now?

I mulled over the new information, fighting against the logical half of my brain that screamed this was a very *very* bad thing. Listening instead to the twisted little minx who whispered in the dark recesses of my mind that that shit was *badass.*

J had the sneaking suspicion I should get out of town. I only stayed in one place for a week or two at a time anyway and I'd had my fill of this place. Besides, it was about time I popped by the house to check on things.

The dead streets made for an easy retreat. I'd dumped vamp number two in with his buddy—though, regretfully, I'd only had the one rose. They would have to share. Just this once though, I didn't want any of the other bloodsuckers to think *The Black Rose* was getting lazy. I found myself grinning again as I heaved my duffle into the back of my old black ford pick-up.

I couldn't help it. The nickname made me feel, I don't know, special? No, that wasn't the word. *Infamous.* Yes, that was it.

I assumed it had something to do with my long

shining black hair, the black leathers I wore while I hunted, and the fact I left a rose—a signature of sorts—with each of my kills. Though I never really left any alive to go blabbing, so, it was likely less to do with my appearance and more to do with the roses.

Beautiful as the rose you were named for, my mother used to say to me when she was upset at something I'd done, *but with more thorns than any flower.* What would she think of me now? Since I'd discarded the petals and embraced the thorns?

I'd like to think she was proud.

It was her I did this for.

After he tore out her...*no.* I wouldn't think about that right now.

I had places to be. More vampires to kill. If my gut instinct was right, they would be after me, now.

They're coming for you, he said before I drove my stake through his heart. It's possible he was lying. Knowing he would die and wanting to thoroughly shake me. To scare me before he met his end. But I didn't think so.

The jingle of the bells atop the door pierced my thoughts and I turned to find the motel manager coming out from his office, rubbing the sleep from his eyes. His stained undershirt lifting at the waist to expose a rotund belly covered in curling black hair.

"Hey there," he called. I ignored him, tossing my sling purse into the cab and getting inside after it.

Feeling around in the dark for my keys. "Just where do you think you're off to?"

His grubby fingers came to rest on the ledge of my open window. The damned thing stopped rolling up a few days ago. I really needed to get that fixed. But when you lived most your life on a night-time schedule, options were limited for a decent mechanic.

"Out of here," I told him, sighing. "Let go of my truck."

"Uh-uh," he chastised, somehow managing to look down on me even though he had to peer up to meet my haughty stare. "You ain't paid yet, miss."

I made an annoyed sound in my throat and reached across my lap for my purse. Under normal circumstances I'd just compel him. Tell him to forget I was ever even here. But I had the extra cash this time. Might as well pay up for once.

"*Or*," he said, drawing out the word as I reached into my stolen wallet for a few hundreds. "We can work something else out if you're short on funds," he said with a sly grin, fingering the thick dark mustache above his thin upper lip.

I don't know why I have faith in any *species anymore...*

I knew I wasn't hard on the eyes. Blessed with perky B's and an ass that won't fit into most jeans—I was soft in all the right places and hard in all the others from too many hours spent training. Add those to the fact that my ever-so-slightly-slanted amber eyes say *fuck me* even when I want them to say *fuck off* and I end up fending guys off most everywhere I go.

But usually the scar over my neck turned them off. The thick white line of slightly raised scar tissue spoke of what I'd been through. What I'd survived.

But fuck if it wasn't ugly as hell.

My usual hunting attire covered it, but normal clothes didn't. I couldn't wait until fall so I could start wearing thick scarves and turtlenecks again without sweating my ass off.

"Listen," I said, locking my gaze on him as I latched onto his mind. Letting the power of my compulsion lace my words. It was *so* much easier with humans. "Have I got your attention?"

He regarded me with a slack jaw. Enraptured the moment my compulsion took hold. He nodded.

"Good. You are going to let go of my truck, turn around, and walk back into your office and forget I was ever here. Then tomorrow you're going to find yourself a nice church—proclaim yourself a born-again Christian and take a vow of celibacy that you *will* uphold for the rest of your miserable life. Oh! And you'll shave that godawful mustache."

I paused for a breath. It wasn't my most creative of punishments, but I was tired, and it would have to do. He wouldn't be harassing any other young girls after tonight and that was the main thing.

"Now go."

With a haze over his eyes and a zombie-like walk, he staggered back to his office.

Pig.

I found my keys and turned over the engine, relief flooding me when it turned over the first time. It'd been touch and go with 'ol Betty for a while now, but I knew she'd pull through. "That's my girl," I whispered to my truck, patting her weathered dash. "Time to go home."

THE DRIVE from the small town where I'd been to my hometown of Silverton, just an hour outside Portland took nearly until dawn. I couldn't remember if I'd adjusted the dash clock the last time I crossed back into Pacific time, but if I had then there was exactly one hour and forty-eight minutes until it would cast its glow over the hills, painting the tops of the tall firs and pines in shades of gold and amber.

I itched for it. The whole drive I'd had a wisp of that familiar hair-raising feeling. What happened with vamp number two earlier must've really shaken me. It felt like the vamp himself was following me home instead of just his words.

A long swallow of the now-cold coffee I'd picked up along the way helped to shake off the feeling, bringing my focus back to the road and home.

Silverton hadn't been home since what happened

with mom—since the men in suits came and took me away. They threw me into the foster care system, and I stayed there until I was sixteen. Then I ran.

My ability manifested young, but it hadn't truly blossomed—become the tool I use it as today until I was firmly in my teen years. I'd have left sooner if I could've.

But somehow, even now, driving down to Silverton always felt like going home. Like even if my mind repelled the memories, or the majority of them were made before I had the brain capacity to capture them forever—my *bones* still remembered. A warmth settled into them. A sort of peace.

I came to check on the house every time I came within reasonable driving distance. Sometimes I stayed a night or two—but that was rare. I couldn't stand the sight of her things still hanging in the closet. The smell of her perfume in the bathroom seemed like it would never fade. So, usually I only stayed long enough to dust and sweep. Make sure no animals had gotten in. No squirrels or raccoons had made a nest in the attic like they did last summer.

And then I would leave again. Back on the road. More pavement to chew. More vampires to kill.

Once I had dreams of going back to school. Getting a degree. But I knew it wasn't me. Would never be me. *This* was what I was meant for. The rest of humanity lived in ignorant bliss of the monsters who thrived right under our noses. Someone had to do this—to beat them back into the shadows. Or else what would happen if we let them keep growing in number?

Would their population one day overtake our own?

What would become of us then?

I pulled into the cul-de-sac, my headlights passing over the brick exterior of the house, and the houses to either side, bumping when I hit the pothole that'd been there for years. Yet somehow, I always forgot to avoid the damned thing. "Sorry, Bets," I said to the truck, turning back the key and bringing her to rest on the street in front of the house.

My heart twinged at the memories trying to claw their way to the surface. I ignored them—shoved them safely away where they wouldn't hurt. I didn't dare look at the other houses—the three I knew inside and out—the ones that once held familiar faces but were now inhabited by strangers. My hands tightened on the wheel and I drew in a long, calming breath that came back out as more of a sigh.

Getting out, I pulled on my sling purse and gave my legs a good long stretch, lifting my hands above my head and bending in either direction. I'd have to do a bit less driving for a while, I didn't think my back could take much more of it. Betty's seats were unforgiving leather, the cushion beneath beat to shit so it felt more like you were sitting on wooden planks than car seats.

Careful to close the door quietly, I approached the

house, feeling the hair on the back of my neck prickle even though there was no breeze. There was a *wrongness* to the place. I knew this feeling.

A vampire was nearby.

Godfuckingdamnit.

Really?

Couldn't a girl sleep?

The houses around mine were all dark and silent. Their curtains drawn for the night. Not even the early risers would be up yet. Good. No witnesses. But I supposed I should try to find some form of cover before the vamp decided to come and attack me. The cul-de-sac was always quiet traffic-wise, but the road outside tended to get busier in the daylight.

Moving into the shadow of the wide apple tree in the front yard, I waited, unsheathing a stake from my thigh. Ready to get the killing over with so I could sleep. I'd toss the body into the shed for now. Bury the leech in the backyard tomorrow night when the town went back to sleep. I wouldn't have enough time to do it tonight.

I stepped around the rotted apples in the overgrown lawn. Their sweet, rotten smell cloying at my nose, and took a fighting stance in the shadows.

"Well if it isn't little Rosie Ward," the deep baritone shattered the stillness. Broke through the barriers of my mind and went straight for my heart.

The hand holding the stake shook, just for a second.

I knew that voice. And there was only one asshole with balls enough to call me Rosie. He'd been calling me that since we were eleven years old.

No fucking way.

I stepped out from the tree's shadow and into the narrow driveway of the house, my feet nearly tripping over bits of loose concrete. "Frost?"

"The one and only," he replied, and I saw that he was alone—leaning against the post of the lean-to covering part of the drive. "You look so different," he added offhandedly.

Different good or different bad? I wondered, my pulse thrumming from a different sort of rush.

Camden Frost lived in the house next door to me growing up. Him and me—and Ethan and Blake, the other boys in the neighborhood—had been completely inseparable. I hadn't seen him, or any of them, since...

Since the day my mother died, I realized, my chest squeezing painfully.

"I—" I wasn't sure what I was going to say, but the sentence died in my throat. *I missed you?* It was true. I did. After they took me away, I hadn't been able to contact them. And years later, when I returned, they had all gone. Moved away. I thought they'd forgotten about me.

What the hell was he doing back here after all these years? Am I dead?

Hallucinating?

I had to be imagining this. I'd pictured exactly this happening too many times to count. I'd hoped for it. Dreamed it. If I was being honest it was part of the reason I still came back to this place—why I never sold the house, even when I got offers double asking price.

Frost's eyes grazed over the scar on my neck and I saw something in his eyes darken, a profound sadness settling over his immaculate features.

"We've been looking for you."

We? My stomach did a little flip. Were the others here, too, then? Ethan and Blake. The desire to see them had me shifting my eyes in all directions, hunting for them among the trees, parked cars, and other houses.

I froze as that same hair-raising feeling swept over me again. I remembered suddenly why I still clutched a metal stake in my hand. A flood of adrenaline crashed into my bloodstream.

They weren't safe here.

I dug the house keys out of my sling bag and tossed them to Frost. "Get inside," I hollered at him, sheathing my stake, hoping he hadn't seen it. I didn't want to freak him out.

They probably heard the rumors. That Rose Ward had gone psycho. How she claimed her mother was killed by a vampire. That the same vampire almost took her life, too. Once the slit in my throat had healed to the point I could speak, it was the first thing I said, tearing up from the pain of trying to talk.

They told me I imagined it. That I was under stress. Grieving. In shock. They labeled me with all kinds of words I didn't understand. But still I screamed *It was a vampire. I saw him. I saw him! I know what I saw!*

Until the threat of permanent institutionalization shut me up.

If I told Frost I needed him to get inside because there's a vampire out here that needed killing and I'd just be a few minutes while I staked the bastard—well, he would think the rumors were true.

And he would leave me again. Just like everyone left me.

Call me raving mad and tell Ethan and Blake I was crazy. That they shouldn't have come to find me at all.

The dark thoughts made it difficult to breathe.

"Why?" Frost asked, catching the keys in one hand, his brow quirked.

His shock of white-blond hair gleamed in the moonlight, almost seeming to glow from within.

"There's something I need to take care of real quick and then we can talk. I...I missed you. It's—well, it's good to see you, Frost." I offered him a tired smile and stepped a bit closer, ready to corral him inside if I had to. I looked left and right, trying not to draw too much attention to the fact that I was checking the rooftops for attackers. "Are Ethan and Blake here, too?"

"No," he replied, not making any movements to go inside like I asked him. Stubborn as always. But I relaxed a little knowing he was the only one out here when there was a vampire lurking somewhere in the shadows. Probably watching us. Listening.

He twirled the keys around his pinkie finger, a look of amusement crossing his ruggedly handsome features. *Fuck,* he aged even better than I thought he would.

I licked my lips, feeling a burn somewhere low in my belly. An ache spreading as I took in the wide expanse of his shoulders and the hard planes of his chest and stomach beneath the too-tight black tee he wore. The way the leather jacket he had over top strained against the swell of his biceps as he continued to fiddle with my keys.

Later, I told myself. I could ogle him all I wanted once he was safe inside and the vamp was dead.

"Who are you looking for?" he asked, catching me glance behind him. "Expecting company?"

I shook my head. "No, I—um—"

There was the grating sound of metal on metal and then the flap of a tarp lifting. Faster than I could blink the vampire had climbed out of my truck bed and cleared the twenty-five paces to me.

How?

But I didn't have time to wonder. I barely had time to grab the stake from between my legs. I'd just gotten it out when the vampire stopped dead no more than three feet away from me, his face stuck in a horrified wide-eyed, slack-jawed silent scream—just out of reach of my stake.

His body buckled. Blood trickled in a stream from his lips. His eyes, a deep blue, were filled with shock. Fear.

The fuck?

It took my mind a second to catch up to what my eyes were seeing. The hand clamped tightly on the vamp's shoulder. My keys still hooked onto the pinkie finger. And when the vampire fell lifeless to the pavement—there was Frost...standing behind him, his fangs bared, the stowaway vampire's bloody heart clutched in his fist.

3

"Oh god," I gasped, dropping the stake to the ground, my hand moving to cover my mouth —to try and stifle the horror making my eyes well with hot tears.

Frost dropped the mangled heart to the ground and bent low to wipe his hand off in the grass by the side of the driveway. "Sorry, Rosie. Didn't mean to scare you."

Didn't mean to...what?

I couldn't speak. Didn't know what to say. I wanted to pick up my stake. Or draw the other one. But I couldn't defend myself against Frost...could I? I couldn't hurt him, not after what he did for me all those years ago—what they all did.

"Don't look so surprised," he said after a few more beats of silence that stretched on like years between us. "By the look of that stake there," he said, his fangs retracting as he glanced down to where the chunk of metal rested in the grass. "I'd guess the rumors are true," he trailed off.

"What?" I managed, still trying to rectify what I was seeing with the Frost I remembered. The thirteen-year-old who had a reputation as a bad boy, but who I knew had one of the biggest hearts of anyone I'd ever met.

And now that heart no longer beat.

No.

"The Black Rose?" he asked. "Did you come up with that yourself or did they come up with it for you?"

My spine straightened and my adrenaline kicked back in, bringing heat back to my tingling extremities. "So, you're here to kill me, then?" I said, deadpan, my fingers itching to draw my stake.

It was true after all. They were coming for me like the vampire warned.

Frost tilted his head this way and that, gave a small shrug. "There's a bounty on your head, Rose. Half a mil."

He must've seen my eyes widen because he barked a rough laugh and ran a hand over his hair, shoving the bit that was longer in the front back into place. "I'd be lying if I said the money wasn't tempting, Rosie," he said, and this time my nickname leaving his lips was a lash across my heart. "But that's not why I'm here."

Frost moved in a blur, faster than even the fastest

vamps I'd seen. Of course, he'd make a magnificent vampire. He was good at everything he did back when I knew him, too. I drew the stake, holding it low at my side, a warning I hoped he didn't realize was a bluff.

Even if he lunged, could I strike him? My childhood friend. My savior.

I can't.

"They say you're good," he said, his voice like warm honey. "So good that you've never left a single one who's seen you alive. They don't even know if you're a woman or a man. Or that you're human. Only that you leave a rose behind."

My throat went dry. I wanted to say something to make him stop moving closer—to stop making me back slowly away from him. To make him go away and never come back. I couldn't stand to see him like this, and I wanted to tell him that, but I couldn't. My throat was full of razorblades and my head full of cotton. I could do nothing more than soak up each and every one of his words.

"But we knew," he continued. "The Black Rose," he repeated. "It had to be you. You dropped off the face of the earth. No record of your death. No record of where you were. And the trail of bodies always lead to within driving distance of Silverton. You always come back here—and that was your mistake. Maybe no one else would've noticed, but when Ethan noticed we figured it out."

He was so close now I could reach out and touch him. Stake him. But my hand trembled with the cool metal in it. My teeth clenched tight.

Fuck. Fuck. Fuck.

He reached out and I flinched, his hand covered my hand on the stake, pushing it away. "We knew it had to be you. When you were in the hospital—we came to see you. They wouldn't let us in—we weren't family."

The smell of him washed over me. Cloves and leather mixed with the spicy tang of aftershave.

"But we heard you," he said. "Screaming. You said it was a vampire. They thought you were crazy, but we didn't. We saw him, too. Just for a second, but we knew you weren't lying."

Oh god. This was my fault. Frost went looking for answers. I imagined how it all played out after I'd been taken away. The three of them enraged that no one believed me. Resolute on finding proof to vindicate me —to prove that I wasn't lying. It would be the sort of thing they would do. For me.

Because we were one, the four of us. If someone fucked with one of us, they faced the wrath of all four. And they'd gone looking for proof and found it. Now Frost was going to be paying for it for the rest of his immortal life.

"I'm so sorry," I murmured, my heart breaking. "The others, are they…?" I couldn't bring myself to say it.

Were they vampires, too?

Frost nodded once and it was like someone was strangling me. I hunched forward, trying to catch my breath. My stomach heaved, but I managed to keep the bile at bay.

Could this be?

It wasn't fair. Not them. Not my boys.

The tears were flowing in earnest now and Frost set a hand on my back. I staggered away, lifting the stake again—a reflex.

"I'm not going to hurt you—" he started, his hand up in a gesture of peace, hurt crossing his features.

In an instant I went from heartbroken to seething mad. This was their fault. They should have let it be. Why did they have to be such *idiots?* So goddamned stubborn! "Fuck you," I hissed at him, but the words came out broken instead of strong like I intended.

"Fuck you, Frost," I tried again and swallowed, trying to relieve the burn at the back of my throat.

"There's the Rosie I remember," he said in a jubilant voice. "Full of piss 'n vinegar, just how I like you."

I shoved him hard in the chest, and he recoiled, stumbling a step back. "Stronger than I remember, though," he added with an even wider grin. The bastard was *enjoying* this.

Could I believe him? Was he really not going to hurt me?

I kill vampires for a living, my mind whispered. And

27

he knows it. *We're basically mortal enemies now.* I grimaced at the thought.

"What do you want then? Why the hell are you here, Frost?"

The adrenaline that spiked only moments before began to wane, replaced with a heavy exhaustion that made my body wilt under the pressure of it. My body sagged and I dropped the other stake, knowing full well I wasn't going to use it.

He narrowed his gaze at me, his river-green eyes confused. His mouth puckering in distaste or maybe confusion. "I'm here for you, Rose. To help you."

My mouth fell open. He was...what?

"Now come on," he said, rolling his shoulders as he changed the subject, as though what he'd just said made any sense at all. He gestured to the heart and corpse still leaking blackish-red fluids all over my mom's lawn. "Help me get him to the shed. We'll have to bury him tomorrow."

---

4

*D*espite how tired I'd been less than an hour before, by the time Frost and I finished hosing off the grass and pavement and lugging the dead vamp into the shed, I was wide awake.

Filled with anger and sadness. About Frost and Ethan and Blake. But also angry with myself for being so stupid, and for not listening to my gut. That whole damned ride from middle-of-nowhere-ville to Silverton I'd felt that charge in the air. I'd chalked it up to what'd happened earlier still irking me when really there was a fucking vampire in my truck bed.

He must've snuck in while the manager of that nasty motel was distracting me. I was smarter than that.

If Frost hadn't jumped in when he did, would I have

been fast enough to stop the vampire? Or had Frost just saved my life for the second time.

Godfuckingdamnit.

As if I didn't already owe him enough.

"This place hasn't changed much," Frost said, taking a look around the main floor of the house.

It really hadn't changed *at all*, but I wasn't about to correct him. I could barely look at him. Holding a conversation without screaming would be impossible.

"Mhmm," I mumbled, following him at a distance as he turned the corner from the kitchen into the living room and made to go upstairs. My face heated as he pushed open the door to my room, the hinges creaking and groaning. I'd have to remember to grab the greaser from the truck and fix that.

My room was the only one I'd bothered to change at all. I'd swapped the power rangers bedsheets for simple black ones with a matching comforter. I'd also taken down most of the band posters but left the ones that were still favorites. My closet was emptied and filled with a few of my extra leathers and some regular street clothes that fit my new adult curves.

But Frost wasn't looking at any of that, he was focused on the corkboard over my old white desk. I hadn't touched that. I couldn't, no matter how much I missed them—or how angry I'd been when they never came for me...

I couldn't erase them. The burning started in my

throat again as I moved to stand next to my best friend, trying to forget that he wasn't the same as I remembered him. That the Frost I knew was dead, and the *thing* standing next to me was not him.

We looked at the messy collage of photos together. My lips quirked at one of the four of us at the lake. I'd taken the photo, but I saw Frost and Ethan in the water, and next to them, midair with eyes wide and teeth bared was Blake after he'd jumped off the thirty-foot cliff.

"I remember this," Frost said with nostalgia in his gaze and a soft voice. His gaze hard. "You looked so beautiful that day. I remember thinking that I'd never feel about another girl the way I felt about you."

In the photo was me. Alone. In a pretty blue dress with white flowers in my hair. It was Frost's mom's wedding to the asshole she ended up divorcing only a few months later. Her third divorce, I think. He'd invited me when the other guys couldn't go, making sure to tell me *this isn't a date, so don't expect me to dance or anything, k Rosie?*

"That's not fair," I choked.

I didn't want to hear that. Not now. They were my best friends, but I loved them all. When I imagined my wedding someday—before all the terrible awful things happened—I'd alternate their faces in my mind where the groom would stand.

Like any eleven-year-old girl—I was hopelessly in

love with my best friends. Except where most girls my age had a crush on one boy, I couldn't choose just one of them. I couldn't imagine my life without even one of them. But as it turned out, I would be forced to live a life without any for the next ten years.

And now…

A tear fell from my eye and dropped onto the desk. Catching the glimmer of wet in the glow of early sunrise coming in from the window a few feet away, Frost turned to me. "I'm sorry," he said, and reached toward my face.

I shrank back. Wanting to hit him and hug him and *stake him* all at the same time.

He tried again, and this time I let him. His thumb wiped the hollow beneath my eye, drying the wetness there before his hand moved lower to trace the curve of my jaw and tilt my face up by my chin. "I will *not* hurt you, Rose. I promise."

How could he promise that? Vampires were creatures of whim. Of unchecked desire. They fucked and fed and killed as they pleased. Out of all the supernatural races, they were the ones with the least control.

I couldn't hold it in anymore. A sob racked my body and my knees tried to buckle. Frost pulled me in, and I didn't fight him. He crushed me against him, and my fingers dug into his jacket, clutching him to me as I cried.

"Shhhh," he hushed me, a hand holding tightly against my lower back. "It's alright."

I shook my head against his shirt, staining it with my tears. "Nothing is alright."

This wasn't me. I couldn't even remember the last time I cried. Years. It had been *years* since I allowed myself the luxury of succumbing to my sorrow. I was The Black Rose. I didn't fucking *cry*.

But I'd missed him. So much. And if I just pretended, he was still just Frost—*my Frost*—it made everything alright. Less painful. I could let him hold me, stroke his fingers through my hair. I could feel his body against mine and feel *rooted* for the first time since mom died. Our arms like the branches of a gnarled tree. One that would stay standing despite storms and floods and age.

I'd forgotten what that felt like. To *belong* in a place. With a person.

"Come on, we should talk," he said, pulling away and leaving me cold and near shivering. My arms crossing to keep warm. "I'm sure you have a lot of questions. And when you're satisfied I'm telling the truth—I have a proposition for you."

My brows narrowed.

"And if you agree, I'll take you to the others."

My pulse jumped. "Blake and Ethan?"

"Yes."

I was shocked at how much I still wanted that—even knowing what they were now. My chest ached with the need to see them. I wanted to touch Ethan's soft brown hair—I wondered if he still wore it long? And to see the spark in Blake's near-black eyes when the light hit them just so. Like snowflake obsidian—the stone I wore in a simple silver setting on my middle finger.

I drew in a long, shaking breath and attempted to stand up straight. "Alright. Let's talk."

"THE FIRST TIME we actually found one was a couple years back—in St. Louis."

I'd been right. After what happened to me and mom, they'd started researching, and then when they were old enough—they went looking for proof. Ethan even went so far as to put himself through *Paranormal Studies* at some swanky university after he finished high school. It made my heart both light and heavy to know they'd never forgotten me like I thought they did. They did the opposite.

They'd dedicated their *lives* to proving I wasn't a liar —and to finding me. But I didn't want to be found. I did my best to never leave a trail. Never stay in a place for more than a couple weeks. Less when I started killing multiple vamps a night. They didn't have a hope in hell of finding me.

"We freaked out," he said animatedly, running a

hand over his hair. The sun had risen fully now, but I'd duct-taped cardboard over my windows and drew the curtains, ensuring not even a sliver of light got inside.

"We saw him in action. We tracked him through his kills—turned out he liked to pick up girls from a club. One night we followed him and his latest victim outside, and then when they got into a car and we followed that, too. He took her to a cabin in the woods and—" he paused. "Well, I'm sure you can imagine the rest."

"So…what? He caught you? Turned you all?"

Frost shook his head. "Nah. We killed him."

That's my boys.

"So then how did you—" I started, and Frost looked away. "What happened to you?"

I didn't think I wanted to hear it, but I needed to. He said he was here to help me. And that I could trust him. There was no way of that happening unless I knew everything.

"You're not going to like this part," he said, his gaze flickering to meet mine for an instant before he looked away again.

I waited.

"We—well, we asked for it."

I shot to my feet. "*You what?*"

I must not have heard him right.

He reached out to grab my hand—no doubt trying

to make me sit back down. I wrenched it out of his grasp. "Rose—"

"Explain," I growled, unflinching.

How could they?

I watched his adams apple bob in his throat and I wondered in the back of my mind if he was growing thirsty…and then I knew what my next question would be.

He bowed his head. "It took all three of us to kill that first one," he told me. "And we barely made it out alive. Ethan had three broken ribs. My skull was fractured. The fucking thing tore a gash eight inches long in Blake's chest."

I sat back down, my hands knotting tightly in my lap.

"It was that night we realized they can fuck with your head."

"Compulsion," I whispered, imagining some vile bloodsucking creatures compelling my boys. My fist clenched and I itched to stab something.

"Yes. Compulsion," he sighed. "It changed our plans. We realized that even if we somehow found a way to prove it. They could make it all go away. If we showed the police a vampire corpse—other vampires would just cover it up. We thought about videotaping one and trying to sell the footage to a news team. But that sort of thing can be manipulated. Or people would just think it was staged."

I was nodding along with his words. These were all things I had thought of in the beginning too, until I figured out what needed to be done.

"So, we figured the only way to make up for what happened to you and Mrs. Ward was to kill as many as we could."

I found myself reaching out to him. I was so fucking proud. Felt so...loved.

Frost looked at me with an apology in his gaze. A rare expression for him. My Frost was never sorry. "But we couldn't do that if we risked dying every time we tried."

It was starting to click in my head. I was strong. I'd trained for years. And I had something they didn't—I could compel, too. But them—they wouldn't stand a chance against a fully-matured vampire as mere mortals. It would be suicide. Come to think of it, I was shocked they'd even survived their first encounter.

"Once we knew they existed, we couldn't go back to our normal lives. How could you, right? But if we were going to be able to do anything about it—we needed to be stronger and faster," he exhaled long and low. "It made sense, in a fucked-up sort of way. They wouldn't expect us to kill our *own* kind."

So, they traded their souls—*their beautiful souls*—to become the monsters they hunted.

To avenge *me*.

It was a little much to swallow, and my stomach soured, bile rising again.

"So, you're saying that you and Ethan and Blake—you're vampire hunters? Like me? Vampires who kill other vampires?"

He shrugged, nodding. "The ones who deserve it."

I cocked my head at him. "The ones who *deserve* it?" I asked him, repeating his words back to him—imploring him to see where he went wrong in that sentence.

"We've been living among them for a year now, Rose. They aren't all monsters."

"*Ha!* Yeah right."

Frost's gaze never faltered. His river-green eyes drilled into me, with not even a flicker of doubt. "It's true. Though I suppose it depends on your definition of monster."

"Next you'll be telling me you live off strawberry milkshakes and have sleepovers with all your vampire besties."

The corner of Frost's mouth twitched up into that crooked half-smile he was known for—the one all the girls in school once drooled over. But he'd never looked at any of them. He only looked at me.

"Blood bags," he said simply, and I shut up, confused, but listening carefully now. "We tried animal blood, but it doesn't make us as strong as the blood of humans does. We can't afford more disadvantage than we already have because of our age. We can live off it in a pinch, though…anyway," he said, switching back to what he was saying before. "We take the blood bags from blood banks, I compel them so it's like we were never there—which is bad enough as it is, we know— but it's better than taking lives."

I had to make sure I was getting this straight. I was still having trouble wrapping my brain around the fact that they didn't kill people to comprehend that Frost could compel, too. It was rare for a vamp as young as he was, still a babe compared to most. But then…he was always the strongest of us.

Pursing my lips, I considered what he said, needing clarification on just one thing before I let him continue. "So, you're a vampire who drinks from a blood bag for sustenance. Ok, I can see that. It makes sense," I said. And it did, but mostly because my mind couldn't comprehend the thought of Frost actually *killing* someone. "But you're telling me you've *never* killed anyone?"

His expression darkened and I saw a muscle in his jaw twitch. "I didn't say that."

"I mean—vampires don't count," I said in a rush, eager for him to take back the four words he'd just let slip from his lips. Surely, he didn't mean—

Frost regarded me with a dangerous flash in his eyes, and for a brief instant, I saw the monster that he kept caged inside. I saw Frost the vampire. And my heart stilled in my chest.

"I'm not talking about vampires, Rosie. I've killed people, too. In the beginning—the urges…they were *unfathomable.* I—I…" he trailed off and I could tell he was having trouble getting the rest out. Hell, I would too if I were admitting to fucking *murder.*

"You *what* Frost?" I was almost shouting now, wanting—*no*—needing him to admit it. That he's fucked up. Him and the other had turned themselves into monsters.

"I'll have to live with that for the rest of my life."

I didn't want to feel sorry for him, but somehow, I did. Maybe it was because I'd spent so long alone. Or maybe it was because I missed him. Or because it wasn't just vampires I hated, but humankind, too.

Regardless of the reason why—the fact that it didn't bother me as much as it once would have made me feel sick. I didn't want to talk about this anymore. I stood back up from the edge of the bed and swayed. My head filled with air. Or something more like helium.

I blinked to clear the black spots crowding my vision and steadied my feet. I needed some water. Or food. Yes, that was it. When was the last time I'd eaten?

"Where are you going?" Frost asked with a gentleness that was so unlike how I remembered him. "You've asked your questions, woman. Now it's my turn to tell you—"

"Unless you want me to pass out, I've gotta eat. Humans need food, remember?"

My hand closed around the handle and in a flash, Frost was off the bed and had himself plastered to the wall behind the door, hissing as a wide swath of sunlight entered the bedroom from the window in the hallway.

"Christ, Rose!" he cursed.

"Sorry," I shrugged, glaring at him and I'd admit—kind of enjoying the sight of Camden Frost cowering behind my bedroom door. "I'm not accustomed to having vampires in my bedroom."

5

*B*lack Betty fired up on the second turn of the key. I wondered if Blake was still good with cars? Maybe he could make my Betty run like new if—

But I couldn't think that far ahead yet. I still didn't know what Frost wanted—what his *proposition* was. If he meant what he said about not hurting me, then I could decline. Walk away scot free.

Was that what I really wanted, though?

He's a vampire! One part of me shouted. *Stake him!*

He's Frost. The other part pleaded. *He's still Frost.*

And he doesn't kill people…at least, not anymore if he was to be believed. That was something, wasn't it?

And fuck if the mere sight of him hadn't done things to my body I hadn't felt in longer than I remembered. I had the occasional lay, sure. Once every few months when I forgot to charge my loyal Mr. Dickins.

But this had been something different. I *wanted* him —or at least, I did before he showed his fangs.

I shook my head as I took the bend onto the main road a bit too quickly, Betty jolting to make the turn. My black hair fell around my face and I batted it out of the way, peering back at the last second to see the cardboard still in place over my upstairs bedroom window.

I smirked. He wouldn't be going anywhere. Not anytime soon. I checked the dash clock. Sunset wasn't for another ten hours and forty-five minutes. Good because I'd need more than a quick drive to Cool Bean Café to work through everything Frost told me. I needed a damned nap, too. And afterward, a nice hot shower and a quad-shot americano to get me through the rest of the day and night.

Frost might be waiting a while.

I ate breakfast like a starved coyote. When the waiter came to take my plate before I was finished, I swear I actually snapped at him. I may have growled a bit. Think I scared the poor little bugger half to death. He couldn't have been more than fifteen. And when he noticed the red stains over the shoulder of my halter, he turned a shade close to green.

I didn't bother trying to explain it away. I just told him, weaving the words with the force of my compulsion to run along and get me another one of those awesome buttery croissants I liked. After I was done there, I napped in the truck. Then I showered in the local gym. I didn't even have to compel anyone to get in there. Turns out if you just act like you belong, no one even bothers to question you.

It was a trick I picked up eons ago. Saved me a lot of spent energy compelling people to get the things I needed.

But now here I was, right back where I started. Betty idling on the street outside the house. Me— looking up at the cardboard covered window, grinding my teeth as the sun started to set, casting the long shadow of the apple tree over the drive.

Godfuckingdamnit.

I pounded my palms against the steering wheel, grimacing, before I slumped back against the seat.

You're the motherfucking Black Rose, bitch, get in there and hear him out. Or kill him. Or leave. But fucking decide one way or the other because this shit is pathetic.

My head fell against the round top of the worn wheel and I sighed. The truth was, I didn't want to do any of those things. I just wanted him to shut up—stop saying things that hurt to hear. Swallow his fangs and be the Frost I remembered instead of the Frost he'd become.

But that wasn't an option. Once changed, there was

no way to go back to the way you were. Now Frost could only ever be one of two things; undead or *dead* dead. He couldn't ever be *living*—not anymore.

Ugh... screw it.

Just as the sun dipped below the horizon, I made up my mind and shut off the engine. The door creaked as I lifted up on the handle and shoved the door open with my heel.

"Rose!"

A blur of movement and flash of black and white-blond.

Frost stood outside the door to my truck, his chest heaving as his relieved gaze traveled from my worn leather boots all the way up my bare legs and over the simple black dress that hugged my curves—and eventually, to my eyes.

"I didn't think you were going to come back. I thought you just left…"

The hurt in his gaze was unmistakable.

Leave him?

It became clear very suddenly. Like a break in the clouds during a storm. The moment when the light shines through and illuminates everything in a myriad of color and brightness. I shook my head. How could I leave him? "You never left me."

He just couldn't find me. None of my boys could. Until now. They never gave up on me. So, how could I give up on them?

Frost stepped in closer and brushed the hair back from my face. This time, I didn't shy away from his touch. "And I never will."

"Good," I said, shocking myself with the word. "You fucking better not, Camden Frost."

6

*I*t was too early to bury the dead vamp. Though the cul-de-sac was quiet, it wasn't fully dark yet and there would still be people returning from their evening jobs. I let Frost lead me back into the house—back into my old room, where the windows were covered, and the bedspread smelled like him now.

He'd snatched a bottle from the cabinet above the fridge on our way up—the liquor had probably been there for years. To this day, I still couldn't reach that cupboard. It said five-foot-five on my driver's license, but I'd been in my thick-soled combat boots that day. I was lucky if I was five-three. A mouse compared to the lion that was Frost.

Frost took a long pull of the amber liquid and handed the bottle to me. It was rum. Mom drank a lot back before what happened. I think it was how she dealt with the knowledge that the creatures of the night lived among us—that they could be our neighbors, or night-time shoppers at the supermarket.

My mom and her mom and back and back and back for as long as our family line went on—we could all compel. And we all knew vampires existed. But it wasn't until me that one of us decided to use our weird ability to do something about it.

"So," Frost started, watching me grimace after a deep swallow of the rum.

"So?"

"Are you finished with your questions? Can I tell you why I'm here now?"

Straight to the point like always.

I remembered he had a proposition for me, and I shivered, imagining what it could be. "I have a few more questions," I said, trying to prolong this—if only because I was afraid I wouldn't like what he had to say.

Frost sealed his lips into a firm line—waiting for my next question. The low-lit lamp on my desk across the room was the only light—and the deep shadows played with the sharp lines of his features. I didn't miss the fact he'd taken off his leather jacket sometime during the day. Now his biceps were bare, and I saw how his unblemished skin pulled tight over bulky muscle. The blue veins in his forearms bright against the paleness of his skin.

Fuck, he was beautiful.

I swallowed, setting the rum down on the short night table at the side of my twin bed. "Are you still you?"

He opened his mouth to reply, but I stopped him with a raised hand. "The truth," I almost growled. I needed to know. Had becoming a vampire changed his mind...? Or was he still Frost, just with fangs and an appetite for blood.

His expression soured and his brows drew together as he considered my question carefully. After a few pulse-pounding minutes he lifted his head and replied. "I am—and I'm not."

That was hardly an answer.

He drew in a breath and raked a hand through his hair. "It's like there's me—and there's *it. It* is difficult to control. It wants blood. It's...feral. But I'm stronger than it. It's just a small part of *me* now. But up here," he said tapping against the side of his skull. "It's still all Frost, baby."

A small crooked grin, and I saw him. He was telling the truth.

I hadn't ever wondered what it would be like to fuck a vampire before. But I was wondering now. My eyes roving over my best friend with a hunger I was sure he didn't miss.

"I believe you," I told him, and tentatively reached out to touch his hand. His palms were calloused. My fingers trailed toward his wrist, finding the skin there was smooth as silk. Up and up some more—I scooted a bit closer on the bed to reach the bulge of his bicep, his shoulder, and with gritted teeth, his face.

A day's worth of growth made his jaw rough. I settled my hand over the stubble, looking into his dark green eyes, wondering if he heard the raucous beating of my heart trying to escape my chest. Of course, he could. *He's a vampire.*

His lips parted. "Rosie—what are you doing?" he asked, his own chest rising and falling more quickly now. The hunger I felt mirrored in his burning gaze.

It wasn't just me then. He felt it, too—this undeniable connection between us.

It had been there from the very first moment I saw him. I just didn't want to listen to it. But if he was still the same man I remembered then…

I had the stake out of the sheath—Frost on his back with me straddling his hips—and the cold metal tip aimed squarely at his heart. The metal pressing into the soft cotton of his t-shirt, a second away from drawing blood.

His hands raised and his eyes widened in surprise. I had him. "Rose," he warned, and though I saw traces of fear, there was also something more primal there. He *liked* being dominated. His cock hardened beneath his jeans, pressing against the soft fabric of my satin panties.

I sealed my mouth against the urge to moan. "Can you control yourself?" I asked him, breathless, my voice somewhere between a hiss and a whisper. "Can you promise me that you'll never take another human life again?"

A muscle in his jaw twitched. "I can promise you that I don't *want* to lose control—or take life," he said, his voice straining as I pressed further into his flesh with the tip of my stake in response. It wasn't good enough.

"I can promise you I will never stop *trying* to maintain control—with everything I have."

I realized I couldn't ask for more than that. Just like a drug addict could never promise they would remain clean for the rest of their life—Frost couldn't promise me that he would never again—in his immortal life— lose control.

My hand shaking, I dropped the stake and it rolled from his chest, onto the bed and then clattered down to the floor. The ringing sound of metal on wood was like a dinner bell, breaking us out of our frozen states.

A growl tore from Frost's chest as he yanked me down to him, our lips connecting with a force that was almost painful. Almost. My body came alive as he took a fist of my hair in his hand and the other slid down my back, securing me to him.

With a sharp tug against my hair, he separated our lips for an instant. "Don't *ever* threaten me again."

There was a flash of danger in him. The bad boy I remembered from school. The one nobody crossed. He'd been patient with me. Letting me ask him questions. Answering them as best he could. He didn't chew my head off for leaving him or shoving him or any of the things I'd said—but now he was back to his old self.

And I couldn't be happier to see him that way.

I grinned. "I make no promises," I said, and his dark expression lightened with the twitch of a smile. Then he dipped his head to my neck, and I froze, ready to attack. But he only planted a hot kiss against the raised flesh of my scar. I shivered, a small whimper escaping my lips.

Taking a fistful of his silvery blond hair, I yanked him back up—kissing him with a passion and fury—pouring my pain into him and letting him take away the hurt and the loneliness of years spent without a friend, or anyone to share my time with.

It felt like finding home.

He groaned as I skimmed my teeth over his lower lip and snaked my hand down between us, popping the metal button from the loop on his jean—dragging the zipper down.

"*Fuck, Rose,*" he gasped when my hand found his cock beneath the denim, I marveled at his size, feeling the silky-smooth skin against my palm as I stroked him. His body trembled beneath me. Every one of his muscles tense.

I wondered how hard it was for him not to lose control. How much effort he was exerting to keep the monster at bay. Judging by the pleading look in his eyes and the quake in his limbs—I had to guess it was a lot.

"If this is too much—" I said, breathy, praying he wouldn't ask me to stop.

"No," he growled. "I want it all."

His hand on my lower back lifted my dress and his other drew down, tearing my panties free from my body—baring my wetness to the cool temperature of the room. I sucked a breath in through my teeth and angled his cock up, settling myself onto him slowly at first, allowing my body to adjust to his length and girth, and then all at once he pushed the rest of the way into me. He filled me gloriously, and I shouted out at the pressure and the building of desire in my blood.

My fingernails dug into his chest, trying to find something—*anything* steady to hold on to as he ground his hips against me, his head tipped back in a silent moan of his own.

His big fingers kneaded my hips, gripping so tightly I'd be surprised if there weren't bruises tomorrow. But I didn't care. I could handle bruises. I could handle it all if it meant never having to stop.

Frost urged me to move—pulling me down and forward. I obliged, moving in time with each thrust of him inside of me. I moaned loudly now, the quickening already beginning somewhere deep inside. My sex throbbing with the build-up.

"Not yet," Frost said. "I'm nowhere near finished with you."

Before I could blink, I was on my back and he was above me, his cock still hard and pulsing between my legs. He knew his way around a woman. I grinned.

Frost drew out painfully slow, watching my reaction with a lip between his teeth. A wicked grin split his face just before he plunged back in, forcing the breath from my body. I pulled him close, needing more. Faster.

"Faster," I urged him, begging now, my claws digging into his back, trying to coax him to keep going.

He flicked my nose with his. "Not yet," he told me, "Slow. I need it to be slow."

I saw how hard he was working to keep up his control. And when his lips parted, I thought I saw his fangs begin to lower.

"Slow then," I acquiesced and started to move against him, wishing there weren't layers of clothing between us. I wanted to feel all of him. I wanted his mouth on my breasts and to see the broad expanse of his shoulders uncovered. The rock-hard abs I felt beneath his shirt but couldn't see.

I started to peel back his shirt and he tore it off the rest of the way, never stopping in his slow thrusts. And then the same hand that tore off his shirt ripped a clean line down the middle of my dress, baring me to him fully. He took in the sight of my aching breasts—the small nipples hard and erect.

I glanced at the shreds that had become of my dress laid out on either side of me.

"Don't worry," Frost breathed, quickening his pace between my legs. "I'll buy you a new one."

Before I could reply, his mouth closed over my right breast and my hips bucked. His tongue rolled over the nipple, pressing flat against it and then flicking it over and over in time with his thrusts.

I moved against him faster, forcing him to bend to my desire. I was sure that if I didn't come soon, I was going to lose my mind.

"Frost," I shouted out and his mouth left my breast to silence me with a smothering kiss and he relented, matching my pace. I gripped the back of his neck, holding his body flat against my own. All hard and soft and tight and wet.

I moaned again—loudly—almost screaming.

"Now," he growled against my lips and the command was all it took to undo me.

His back muscles stiffened under my fingers and he came into me. My orgasm exploded through my body, tightening muscle and sinew. Singing in my blood. It consumed me. Black spots bloomed in my vision and I clutched him, the pitch of my moan rising to meet the deep timbre of his replying growl.

"Mine," he said between broken breaths.

I nodded, still dazed—my mind foggy and limbs suddenly heavy. "Yours."

7

I'd sent Frost to get my duffle and lay, still naked, in the bed as he set it down next to me. "The hell you got in this thing?" he asked.

My gaze flicked up to meet him, biting back a smirk. "You don't want to know."

Beneath the few layers of clothes and leathers was an arsenal of weapons. Another set of stakes in case I misplaced mine, and a further pair of wooden ones if I lost those, too. A couple of daggers. A crossbow I was still hopeless at. And my Katana. I was still learning how to use that—but I was dead set on mastering it.

Another way to kill a vamp without plunging a stake in its heart was to remove the head. And my katana was forged by a master in Japan—I'd paid almost two thousand for it and waited the two months for it to be made and shipped all the way here.

It was sharper than a surgeon's scalpel. If he was lucky, maybe I'd show him someday. I dug through the clothes, pulling out a simple shirt and skirt combo. I wasn't a dresses and skirts kind of girl, but it was hard to conceal my stakes when I had to wear the garter and belt over top of a pair of jeans. Much easier to hide them beneath the hem of a skirt or dress. And no one ever expected a girl to store *weapons* up there. At least, not the kind that killed.

I drew out a cigarette and lighter from the side pocket and flopped back onto the pillows, lighting it as I did.

"You smoke now?" Frost crooked a brow.

"Only after a particularly good lay," I said and kicked at him playfully with my heel.

He shook his head, and I followed the trail of his gaze as he carved a path over my still-naked body, settling at the spot between my legs. A soft groan left his throat. "You should put your clothes back on or—"

"Or what?" I teased, maneuvering myself so my legs parted just a little, giving him a full view.

He stopped breathing. "As much as I would love to tear into that again," he said, licking his lips, the gesture made me shiver. "We have to talk. We've been looking for you because—"

"Yeah, yeah," I said, dipping my hand into my nightstand drawer to pull out the ashtray I kept inside. I ashed the cig and turned back to him, crossing my free arm over my chest. *"This proposition,"* I said, giving the words half an air quote with the hand that wasn't covering my breasts from the cool air in the room.

Frost nodded. "That's right."

"I want to see the others," I said, my tone demanding. "Ethan and Blake. I want to see them before I decide. You can tell me together what it is you want."

I was afraid that if I declined, or didn't like what he had to say, I would ruin my chance to see them. Would Frost still take me to them if I denied his request? I wasn't about to risk it. I missed all of them so much. Frost was just a single piece of our puzzle of four souls.

He cocked his head, clucking his tongue as he considered. Annoyance in his expression. "I had a feeling you might say that."

"I don't see what the problem is?"

He sighed audibly, leaning over me to snag the bottle of rum from the nightstand. "They're in Atlanta," he said.

Atlanta? I had been there only a week ago.

"We got word that the Black Rose hit there a couple weeks back, so they've been scoping out the place looking for you."

They were only a week behind me the whole time... it was a crazy thought to know that they were so close to finding me—probably more than once.

When we heard there was a possible Black Rose murder in Oklahoma, they stayed there to keep searching—and I came here. I had this feeling you were on your way home. I couldn't figure out why. I just knew if I came here that you'd find me."

And he'd been right.

I frowned. "But Atlanta is on the other end of the country," I complained.

"I can book us two red-eye tickets for tomorrow night."

Tempting, but. "I won't leave Betty," I told him.

"Who?"

"Betty," I repeated. "My truck."

He looked toward the window as though he could see straight through the cardboard. "Black Betty. Real original, Rosie."

I punched him in the arm. "Don't talk about my Betty like that," I chastised. "She's a one of a kind woman."

"Like her owner."

I sat back, smugly. "Exactly."

"Well," said Frost, his chest expanding as he drew in a long breath. "Let's get the corpse buried out back and hit the road. We've still got a good amount of moon-light to burn. If we leave tonight, we can be in Boise before dawn."

Ha! He underestimated my abilities. You didn't have

to adhere to state traffic laws when you could just convince the officers you'd done no wrong with a few well-chosen words.

I'd have us to Salt Lake City by morning. Easy.

But first, coffee.

8

"*C*hrist, woman!"

I'd just swerved around another transport going grandma speeds down the dark highway. There was only a small window of laneway before oncoming traffic would be on top of us and I'd just made it. Revving Betty's engine to the precipice of what she could handle to get back into our lane before we were hit.

"You know," I said with a sly grin. "For an immortal being, you really are a pansy, Frost."

He guffawed, his hand against his chest as though he were deeply wounded by my remark. "It's not me I'm worried about," he said, exasperated. "How have you survived these last ten years driving like that?"

I shrugged innocently.

Frost underestimated me again. I'd always been a

quick healer. And I swore my bones were denser than most.

Somehow, even being as short as I was, I managed to weigh nearly as much as a body builder with an extra foot of height on him. My mom had been the same. We were just built different. I liked to think maybe we were our own breed. Like shifters. Or Fae. Maybe we were *born* to fight vampires.

I didn't like to consider the alternative—that maybe we were somehow *like them.* Part vampire? Half-dead. Half-living. *Ugh.* I shoved the thought away, shaking off the disgust.

I gestured for Frost to pass me another crème-filled donut. When I reached to take it from his hand, he swatted my fingertips away before I could snag it. "Eyes on the road," he ordered and hand-fed me the thing until all that was left were the crumbs in my lap and a bit of crème on his index finger.

He went to pull away, glancing this way and that—I assumed looking for a napkin—but I leaned forward and took the crème coated digit into my mouth and sucked the sweetness off.

Frost gaped at me—I could see him from the corner of my eye, watching. "What?" I said, feigning nonchalance. "I don't have any napkins."

We sped at breakneck speeds—chewing the

blacktop mile after mile. It became increasingly clear that we weren't going to make it all the way to Salt Lake by sunrise. Maybe I'd been a little cocky back at the house. *But* we did make it well past Frost's suggested daytime stop of Boise and had just crossed the state line.

"We should stop soon," Frost said, and I followed the line of his gaze to see the sky had already begun to lighten. Not much. But enough to know that within the next half hour—the sun would rear its golden head and fry him to a crisp.

I wondered what it was like to always live in darkness. I glanced at my friend and found his expression sad. Distant. A heaviness settled on my shoulders. There had to be some way for him to see the sun again. I'd find a way.

Did he regret it? The question came unbidden to my mind. They'd done this to themselves partly to avenge me.

Was it worth it? I'd be lying if I said I hadn't thought about doing exactly what they did back in the beginning. Before I learned that I could be almost just as fast as them. Nearly as strong. And before my talent to compel fully manifested. I'd been desperate to find the bastard who killed my mom—who almost killed me. I'd almost traded my soul to the devil, too.

"Rose!" Frost yelled, his stony expression shifting to horror.

I swiveled the wheel just in time to miss the parked black sedan on the side of the highway. We bumped along on the dirt at the side of the pavement before Betty's bald tires found the road again.

My spine was erect, and my legs were tingling. My pulse pounded in my ears and blood rushed to my head, giving me a spike of adrenaline. Once we were safely between the two yellow lines again, I burst out laughing. Loud, belly laughing. Tears obscured my vision and my sides ached.

Frost was absolutely horrified, and somehow that just made the whole thing even *more* funny. I pounded my palm on the steering wheel hollering. "*Fuck,*" I exclaimed when the laughter began to subside. "That was a close one."

"Do you have a fucking death wish, Rose? Or are you just in—"

The siren cut through the tension in the cab like a knife. Both Frost and I stilled in our seats as the blue and red lights of the cop car gaining speed behind us blinded me.

"*Shit!*" Frost shouted. "Now look what you did."

I rolled my eyes at him.

"Just pull over and be quiet," Frost said, clearly grumpy now. "Let me do the talking. I'm still not great at compelling, but I can handle this."

He was clearly gearing himself up for it. Head bent as he tried to focus—maybe draw on his ability or collect his energy. I barely remembered when it used to be that hard for me.

Good thing for the both of us, I was good at it. Very good at it. Especially with humans.

"I got this," I said to him as I gently coaxed Betty to a stop at the side of the road and the officer pulled up behind us.

"What?" Frost growled.

I raised my brows at his confusion, forgetting that he likely didn't know I could compel. The vampires who knew of me thought I was a man or maybe another vampire. I didn't leave any alive to go blabbing that I was a human who could compel. Well, except for that one vamp in El Paso, but he was so fast there wasn't any way I could have caught up to him when he set his mind to running away. Slippery fucker.

I reconsidered showing Frost my ability—still not trusting him fully—but thought better of it. Let him see what I can do. How good I am at it. Maybe he'd think twice about how *fragile* he seemed to think I was.

I mean, fuck, how did he think I managed to kill all the vamps? I was a trained fighter, yes, but not a damned ninja assassin.

The officer got out of his vehicle and slowly meandered his way over to my truck, his hand hovering over his weapon. Paranoid much? Though since the truck was occupied by a vampire and a vampire huntress, I supposed I couldn't blame the guy. In this case—he was right to be afraid.

He saw that the window was already down and tipped his wide-brimmed hat. I watched his throat bob in the light pouring over us from his headlights and oncoming traffic. When he lifted his head, my heart sank. A pair of glasses were affixed to his face with a string that connected them on the back of his head— holding the frames tight to his skull.

Well, fuck.

"Evening ma'am," he said, his tone professional, though I didn't miss the slight widening of his eyes when he saw me. My scar was in full view, and his eyes zeroed in on it like a missile on target. I should've been used to it by now, but I still flinched when I saw how his expression twisted for an instant from placid professionalism to horror, disgust, and then finally, as it always did—to pity.

"Evening," I replied, stoic. "Is there a problem?"

It took the middle-aged man a moment to gather his thoughts and tear his gaze away from the ragged edges of my scar. He cleared his throat. "Afraid so," he said. "Do you know how fast you were going?"

My teeth ground together behind my lips. How could I convince him to take those glasses off? Or should I just tear them from his head? Had he called for backup?

When I didn't respond right away—trying to find a

way out of this mess that wouldn't end with a visit to the station, the officer sighed. "License and registration," he said, pulling out a small notepad and pen from his breast pocket.

I passed him the card and document from the little compartment to the left of the wheel.

Frost nudged my leg with his knee, and I swiveled my head to him. His hands were white-knuckled claws gripping the edge of the seat. If he squeezed any tighter, he'd tear chunks right out of them. The fuck was his problem?

I was about to ask him as much when I realized what he was looking at. Down the highway—across the blue sky—the signs of dawn approaching seemed to have sped up. But that wasn't right. It wasn't supposed to rise for another half an hour at least!

Had I adjusted the clock wrong? Miscalculated?

The base of the sky was brighter than it had been only moments before. The reddish-orange glow beginning at the place where the sky met earth on the horizon. Spattering the sky with yellowed clouds. Staining the blue in hues of purple and pink.

The officer was already going back to his truck and I turned to Frost. We needed to get him the hell out of here. My heart jumped into my throat and the hairs on my arms rose. We had maybe ten minutes before the sun crested the horizon. Fifteen at best.

"Rose," he said, turning to me, taking my hand in his. "Look, I just want you to know—"

"Shut the fuck up," I snapped at him, ripping my hand away.

He didn't get to say goodbye to me—not again.

I wouldn't allow it.

I kicked the door open and stepped outside the cab, stomping over to where the police officer was entering my information into his computer.

He caught sight of me—a shadow drawing nearer and bashed his head against the roof of his cab in his haste to stumble out of the black cruiser. "Miss!" he said, reaching again for his gun. "Miss, I'm going to need to ask you to return to your vehicle."

The warning in his voice was clear, but if I knew anything about the inner workings of men—the majority of them didn't feel very threatened by girl who looked like I did. Short and sweet—with my trademark *fuck me* eyes. I didn't stop walking, trusting my gut instinct that he wouldn't shoot.

Even after he drew his gun and aimed it at me.

Even after he cocked it back, the *click* making my skin bristle.

I didn't stop.

When I was close enough, I ran the last two steps, swung out my leg and roadhouse kicked the gun from his hands. It clattered into the dirt and gravel and he moved to retrieve it, but I was there first.

Frost was, too. He kicked the weapon out of the officer's reach at the same time I dodged his swinging fist, clamped my hand around his stubble-covered neck and tore the glasses form his eyes. Shoving him back behind the police vehicle to attempt to block us from the prying eyes of early morning traffic. Thankfully there weren't many people on this highway this time of morning. "Look at me," I ordered him, shouting.

"P—please," he said, his confidence vanishing. "I've got kids."

"Rose! We need to go!" Frost shouted, "Let me—"

"I'm not going to hurt you," I hissed, looking over my shoulder to see the orange glow of the rising sun was spreading faster—too fast. "Look at me!"

Finally, he did. "You never saw us," I commanded. "We were never here. You are going to get back into your car and you're going to go that way," I said, pointing in the direction opposite to the one in which we were headed. "Until sunrise."

Frost was already moving back to the truck, reminding me we were out of time.

"Go," I said and released his throat, running back to the open driver's side door. I jumped inside and slammed the door closed, punching Betty into drive and flooring the gas pedal.

We lurched back onto the road, almost hitting another car before I pulled out ahead of it and hammered Betty down as fast as she could go.

"Rose, where are—"

"There's a motel," I said, the panic in my voice palpable as we passed car after car—a hollow pit forming in the bottom of my stomach. "Near Snowville. Just a few more miles."

"We don't have a few more miles!"

I looked into the emptiness on either side of the road. There had to be someplace else we could go. *Any* shelter would be good enough. But I saw nothing except sparse grass, rolling hills, and dirt. As far as I could see in any direction. I'd been on this highway several times, but I couldn't think of anything except the motel I knew was in Snowville. I knew because I'd stayed there once.

Stupid! Why did I try to go so far? We should have stopped in Boise, or Twin Falls. Fuck, we could have stopped so many damned places along the way if I hadn't been so bent on getting there—seeing the others.

And what would I tell them now. *Hey guys, I missed you—oh and by the way Frost is dead because I'm a huge idiot.*

I was taken aback at how much even thinking about it hurt. Like a knife in my gut. I reached over and took Frost's hand, hot wetness stinging my eyes. "I won't let you die."

He couldn't die. Not after I'd just found him again.

I didn't care if he was a vampire! I wouldn't lose him or any of the others. Not ever again.

Frost offered me a small, tight smile as if to tell me *it's alright, Rosie.*

But it was far from being alright.

I saw a slice of dirt road among the sparse patches of green. Like a ribbon cast from the sky to lay in a curving line through the landscape. It had to lead somewhere. *Roads lead to shelter.*

Releasing Frost's hand, I yanked the wheel hard to the right, Betty skidding from the blacktop, bumping onto the dirt drive. I threw her into a lower gear, and she spat dirt from her rear end as we barreled down the drive. My fingers clutched the wheel until they hurt.

Neither of us spoke as the sun crested the tips of the white-capped mountains far into the distance. But the noise was deafening. The roar of Betty's engine matched the sound of rushing blood in my ears. And the *chink* of stones on Betty's undercarriage and her tires as they ground against the earth—it was a symphony of dread.

"There!" I pointed, almost bouncing in my seat at the sight, just as we turned a bend over a small hill in the drive, we could see it. The long shape of a wooden barn—withered and run down—but with no windows that I could see and a green tin roof that looked like it was newer than the original structure. *Shelter*. It was shelter from the sun.

I *whooped* and Frost leaned over and took hold of my face, planting a rough kiss on my cheek before the creaking groan of his door opening stole my attention and I watched him—a blur of dark and light as he ran full-tilt to the structure just as the sun came over the hills and blinded me with its piercing amber light.

here were a few holes and cracks in the wooden walls of the old barn, but it did a decent job of blacking out the sunlight, and it looked to be abandoned so that was a bonus. There were stacks and mounds of hay in an otherwise empty stall. The dry, pale-yellow straws made an additional barrier— blocking Frost from the touch of even the smallest ray.

He assured me he wouldn't burst into flames if a bolt of sunlight grazed him—he'd have to be standing in full sunlight for that, and even then, the whole process would take a few minutes.

"Hurts like a bitch, though," he said, and I saw where the sun had got him on his neck, just above his collar. He'd been fast in getting to safety, but not fast enough to avoid the rise of the sun entirely. The flesh on his neck was red, raised, and angry. Bits of it blackened as though scorched by the touch of flame. It was already starting to heal, though.

If he were an older vamp, the wound would've closed up and healed within minutes, even seconds.

"Looks like it," I said, wincing. "I'm so sorry, Frost," I added in a rush.

After I'd hopped out of the truck and followed him inside the barn, I'd buried myself in his chest, wrapping my arms tight around him like vises. Afraid if I let go, he would disappear. I'd almost lost him, and the terror I felt had been more real than anything I'd felt since that day ten years ago.

I couldn't remember the last time I'd been properly scared. Fuck, I'd forgotten what that felt like. It was a terrible, bone-wracking, heart-stopping, gut-wrenching feeling I never wanted to repeat.

Frost let me hold him like that for a while before he'd pulled away, whispering to me in a soft voice. "I'm fine."

We'd been sitting in the hay for nearing an hour, and he'd barely spoken. Guilt weighed on me for what I'd done I didn't know what to say. *I almost got him killed.*

Mom always said I'd be the death of someone someday. She'd meant it as a joke. But…what if she was right?

"I'm fine," he said again. "Quit apologizing."

I dropped my head. "I think I have a first-aid kit in the—"

"Did you compel that cop, Rose?"

The question caught me so off guard, it took a moment for me to process it. Our little encounter with the police officer felt like it happened *ages* ago. I'd already pretty much forgotten about it.

Frost grabbed my hand, trying to pull my attention —to make me look at him. When I did, I found fire in his gaze. His nostrils flared. "Did you?"

I licked my cracked lips, wishing I'd had water in the truck instead of coffee all night. Why did he seem so pissed about this? "Yeah," I said, raising a brow at him. He really hadn't known. When he didn't say anything right away, I thought maybe he'd somehow figured it out.

I'd been really bad at it back when we were kids, but he had to have noticed how easy it was for me to convince people to do what I wanted. But not him—or the guys. I never used it on them—at least not on purpose.

I always wondered if my kiss with Blake when I was thirteen and he was fifteen was a product of my compulsion, though. I'd told him to do it. It wasn't a command—I hadn't meant it like that. I just...wanted him to. We were laying on his trampoline—just the two of us—staring up at the sky. When he looked at me—at my lips—I thought he wanted to, so I gave him permission.

But he never kissed me again after that and I always wondered…

"Shit, Rose. How—" he started, but stopped himself, confused and trying to work out the puzzle in his head. To solve the mystery that was Rose Ward.

Good fucking luck…

Even I hadn't figured it out.

"But you're human. How is that possible?"

"Beats me," I sighed.

"Are you sure you're hu—"

"Yes," I snapped. "I'm sure."

Frost recoiled from my tone. "I didn't mean anything by it. Just asking."

"Maybe that's why Raphael wants—" he murmured to himself, as though he'd finally worked out the solution to another problem he'd been trying to figure out.

I cocked my head. "Who's Raphael?"

Frost jerked his head to the right—meeting my gaze. Relaxed his shoulders and slumped against the pile of hay. "No one," he said. "Just a friend."

From his sudden inability to look me in the eye, I knew I'd get no more out of him on the subject. Not right now, anyway. I made a mental note to ask him about it again later. Committing the name Raphael to memory.

A few beats of silence later, I caught Frost staring in

a longing sort of way at my jugular and shivered. "Um, Frost," I said, snapping my fingers in front of his face. "When's the last time you fed?"

Blinking rapidly, he cast his gaze away from me and made a choked, clearing sound in his throat. His voice was hoarse when he said. "A few days."

"That wasn't good."

"I can manage it."

But I could tell he was straining. The color that'd been in his cheeks when I first saw him—that made me think he was human—was gone. His pallor was pale and sickly. And the hoarseness in his voice and vein bulging from his neck told me he was near parched and his control was waning.

"It's just the sunlight," he said, jabbing a finger toward his neck. "It weakened me. And when I'm weakened—"

"You need to feed to recover."

I didn't pretend to have a vast wealth of knowledge about the workings of vampires or any of the supernatural species. It wasn't as though you could google that sort of thing, and I never let one live long enough to have this sort of conversation.

But I was good at putting two and two together. Always able to connect dots, even if they were miles apart.

Frost nodded. "Yep. Basically."

"How much longer can you wait?" I asked him—all

business now. There was a problem—albeit a problem I never foresaw myself having to deal with—that needed solving. I may have to feed a vampire. The thought of letting Frost bite me was so revolting it made me want to barf. But, if I had to, I could hunt him down an animal. Or compel some blood from the nearest hospital.

"The truth," I said before he answered me. "How long?"

"I won't hurt you—no matter how long I have to wait," he growled, and I saw from the hardness in his eyes and the set of his jaw that he believed it.

"I believe you," I told him earnestly, and I did. "But I'm not particularly worried about you attacking me Frost. I can defend myself. I'm worried about other people."

We would be back in the road at sundown, and by then he'd be ravenous. It was possible he wouldn't be able to control himself. "Didn't you bring blood bags with you?" I asked after the only response he gave me was to clench his jaw and seethe quietly.

"I can go a week—sometimes more without feeding," he said. "I trained myself to do it from the start."

My eyes widened. Impressive for a vamp that was barely more than a year old. "But you're injured," I said, willing him to admit to me how badly he needed to feed.

I saw the blackened flesh had healed already a bit

around the edges, but it was eating up all the life and energy he gained from drinking human blood and leaving him starved and weak.

"I can help you, Frost," I said in a gentle voice, not wanting big bad Frost to feel emasculated or like I doubted his abilities. I pulled my cellphone out of the purse I'd fetched earlier from the truck and stood to find a signal, lifting the device high into the air as I watched the bars blink into and out of life. I had one bar—maybe one and half. It would need to be enough.

"What are you doing?" he asked, watching me warily from his nest of hay.

The second bar lit up and stayed steady near the back of the barn and I stilled, pulling up google. *Hospitals near me.* But the nearest one was over an hour away and there was no way to know for certain if they had any fresh blood on hand. The nearest blood bank was even further.

"Would animal blood work?" I asked, thinking I'd need to up my crossbow game if I was going to be able to catch or kill anything of a decent size for him. And that was assuming there were wild animals in this barren wasteland. There weren't even trees here. I'd have to drive several miles to even find an ecosystem that supported the kind of animals I would need to feed him. We were surrounded by dry dirt and highway at the height of drought season.

Godfuckingdamnit.

"It might stave it off long enough," he said—the closest thing to admitting what he really needed.

I tried to think of other options—but there seemed to be only one that I could think of. I shut off my phone screen and gripped it tightly, lowering it, cursing under my breath.

Maybe we could wait. Maybe Frost was right, and he could hold off until we could get to some place with blood that wasn't in a human body—or *my* body.

"Doubt you'd find anything around here, though," he said, mirroring my thoughts.

I went back to the hay-sealed stall and sat with him again, putting an extra couple feet of space between us than there'd been before. Frost noticed—a muscle in his jaw twitching. But he said nothing, sitting in stony silence as we waited for the sun to set.

10

*I*t was only three hours before I started to worry in earnest.

"*Damnit* Frost," I exclaimed after returning from a bathroom break in the shrubbery behind the barn.

He was positively white. Like *ghost-level* pale. He was breathing hard in and out of his mouth, and his hands were clenching and unclenching at his sides. The wound in his neck was almost fully healed, which meant he was likely almost completely depleted of the life-source he used to continue on.

He needs to feed.

The thought was both an admonishment and a horrified scream rebounding in my skull.

"You should leave," he growled, straining. Sweat beading over his brow—his incisors slipping out from his gums. "I can't," he started, but couldn't finish the sentence.

Couldn't look at me, either. He was in pain. And not just the physical kind. Self-hatred and loathing were what he was feeling. I could tell.

It was the same look he had after beating up little Billy Barnes in grade eight. Billy was a bully—he'd punched a girl that day near the end of the school year, and it wasn't the first time he'd done it, either. But Frost hadn't meant to go so far. He hadn't meant to break Billy's ribs.

And for him to spend the summer healing in bed rather than out doing what teenage kids wanted to do over summer break.

In my mind—Billy had deserved it. In Frosts, he was in the wrong. He carried the guilt of his actions through that whole summer. He didn't raise his fists again for months even though there was plenty of opportunity. He had the same look he had now.

Like he hated himself.

Like he was a monster who should be feared. Left to be alone.

I wasn't having it.

"You told me you could control yourself," I said, remembering last night with a growing warmth between my legs and a squeezing sensation low in my belly. "And you did."

He turned to me, his body heaving with the force of

his breaths. His eyes dark and bloodshot. His fangs out fully now.

Fuck.

I couldn't fucking believe what I was about to say. What I was about to *do.*

"Drink from me," I blurted before I could change my mind. Immediately I wanted to cram the words back in and coughed to cover the slight gag threatening low in my throat.

Frost looked at me like I was insane, but I didn't miss the way he swallowed hard and deep, like he was salivating just to have heard me say it. "No."

What?

"I can't have you attacking the first person we come across when the sun finally sets. I won't allow it."

Hands on hips, I stomped across the barn, planting myself in front of where he was sitting, back hunched, elbows on knees. He hissed, shoving himself back as far as he could before he hit hay. "*No, Rose.* I won't do it."

What was it people said about wanting something more once you've been told you couldn't have it? If this was reverse psychology, it was working. My stubborn ass self was rising to the surface, taking over.

"Oh yes you will," I snarled back.

"Please—"

"Just fucking do it, Frost. Get it over with. Just don't take too much or you'll have to drive, and I suspect you adhere to the road laws," I said the last part

ELENA LAWSON

with a roll of my eyes, trying to make him think I didn't care at all about doing this. *Nope. Totally cool. This was totally ok.*

"It'll take us an extra day to get there if I let you drive," I added after he still refused to respond, sitting there like a damned child who was pretending not to listen.

Ok. Fine.

He wanted to play it like that...I could play dirty, too.

Hardening myself, I worked to slow my pulse with a forced aura of calm. *This is a business transaction. It's not really me—I can pretend I'm someone else.*

I only have to do this this one time, and then I'll never have to do it again.

My mouth went dry as I knelt in front of him, brushing my long black hair back from my neck.

"Rose..." he said, his voice a plea.

I tried not to look at his fangs—not to show any trace of disgust.

I leaned in and tipped my head to one side. He shook.

I planted my hands on his legs, pulling myself in closer between his legs. Not giving him any option for refusal or escape.

"Rose..."

I kept my nails filed sharp and painted matte black. I did it so I would always have another sort of weapon on me. I never imagined I would be using my polish-hardened black daggers on myself.

Then again, I never imagined a lot of things that'd happened in the last forty-eight or so hours was going to happen. Sooner or later, I'd have to stop being surprised by the shit life had a habit of throwing my way when I least expected it.

If this was the start—I couldn't imagine what sort of insanity awaited me when we got to the guys and I finally agreed to hear what they wanted from me.

My fingers were steady as I punctured my flesh, dragging the nail down in a vertical slit until the sting of air on the small open wound made me suck a breath through my teeth. The warm wetness of my blood as it bloomed and dribbled down to my collarbone made me wrinkle my nose in momentary disgust.

"Do it Frost," I ordered, and he broke. The monster he hid deep within came out in a flash of hunger crazed green eyes and bared teeth.

With a speed that I couldn't ever match, he had me, one hand clutching at my ribs and the other a fist in my hair as his teeth came down on the soft skin of my neck. His teeth tore into me and pain exploded from the bite.

It took everything inside me not to draw my stakes against him. To keep myself there and let him drink from my artery. But…the pain was fading fast, I realized. And it wasn't until I heard the moaning sound that I recognized it as my own voice. That *I* was moaning.

It felt…good.

Fuck, it felt *so damned good.*

My body was reacting to the bite in ways I never could have anticipated. My breasts hardened and a delicious ache was spreading through my belly, moving out to tickle all my extremities. I found myself touching Frost, trying to draw him in closer. Wanting his fangs in deeper. Harder. Wanting him to take *all of me.*

His grip on my ribs loosened and I almost cried—wanting—no, *needing* him not to stop. Instead of allowing him to let go, I snatched his hand and moved it lower, beneath my skirt—to the burning ache there that desperately needed sating.

I was slick with silky wetness when his fingers brushed against me and my hips bucked as he fingered my opening, biting down harder. The pain mixing with the pleasure in a hot crescendo of sensation that took my breath away. His responding growl told me he was feeling what I was feeling, too.

The desire burned more brightly than anything I'd ever felt before. I knew in that moment if I didn't have him, I would die. Right there in the barn among all the hay and dirt. My heart would just stop beating if I didn't sate this need.

His fingers thrusted into me and my body arched

again, my hands finding the bulge of his cock beneath his jeans. When I opened my eyes for a brief second, trying to find the buckle of his belt, my vision swam.

My fingers were sloppy as they attempted to undo the buckle.

There was a weight on my chest—crushing my lungs. My pulse pounded hard and fast in my ears. I was weakening.

Dying.

In a moment of clarity, I tugged away, and Frost's fangs broke free of my skin.

"Fuck," he exclaimed and fell back as though burned. "Fuck, Rose. I—"

But my body was already working to replace the blood that was lost. Healing itself. The cells multiplying and splitting and multiplying again, as though it was prepared for this.

As my vision cleared and the wound healed, I noticed two things. My pulse still pounded, and the intense wave of desire that had taken hold of me still wasn't sated. Dulled, maybe, but my sex throbbed with the absence of his fingers and my skin prickled with yearning.

"Shut up and take your pants off," I said between clenched teeth.

"Wha—"

"Take. Them. Off."

"But you're hurt—"

Showing him I was far from *hurt,* I stood towering over his sitting form without even a hint of stagger or sway. I flipped my hair back, revealing my neck to him. The itch of the flesh knitting back together had stopped, and I knew the flesh would be closed, a bit pink if anything at all.

"Now take off your pants, Frost."

The hunger was back in his eyes. Mingled with relief. He did as he was told, unbuckling the belt, and then drawing down the fly, setting his cock free.

I didn't waste a minute, tugging my shirt up over my head and tossing it to the floor. My bra followed a second later. Then my skirt. And my panties. I stood there bared to him, nipples rock solid and hair raised with anticipation.

His cock twitched as he took me in, appraising me as if I was a work of art. It was almost as though I could feel the touch of his gaze on my skin. Like phantom fingers. Awakening me inch by inch. Setting my skin ablaze.

I leaned forward and ripped the jeans from his legs, tossing them somewhere behind me before I was kneeling again, this time over top of him, my knees pressing into the hay and concrete as I straddled him.

He shook his head; his hands moving to cup my ass and lift me from the floor until my sex was level with his mouth. My hands found a handhold on a metal ring beneath the hay a few feet above his head. I gripped it with white-knuckled fists as he squeezed my cheeks and took my sex into his mouth.

I shouted, unable to contain the sound or all the roiling heat bubbling up from deep within—threatening to spill over. His tongue flicked against my clit and I felt the press of his fangs against my lips. It was all I could do to hold on to the metal ring and ride out the waves of pleasure radiating over me.

He moved one of his hands between my legs and plunged two fingers inside, adding exquisite pressure to the constant flicking of his tongue. His fingers picked up speed and vigor, plowing into me again and again until I was on the cusp of my release.

"Please, Frost," I begged. "*Please.*"

With a roar he clawed me down from the metal handle and sheathed himself inside of me, my knees slamming against the floor. I cried out, but not at the pain, at the still-building release. At the nearness of it as he thrusted in and in *and in*. Lifting us both from the floor with the force of his fucking, arm around my middle to hold me in place.

His eyes met mine and suddenly the fangs didn't matter anymore. I bent down to taste him, pressing my lips to his hard enough to feel the fangs hidden just inside. The tip of one skated across my lip, drawing a bead of blood he gently sucked away as he continued to drive into me.

Oh god.

Oh god.

I was coming undone. Derailed. A fucking freight train was coming and there was no stopping it now.

"Frost," I choked out a second before I splintered into a thousand pieces of myself, crying out his name. Spiraling down in a tangle of limbs. Of mingled breath, warm flesh and blood. Of spent energy and single heart beating enough for the both of us.

We lay still save for the rise and fall of our breaths. Me utterly spent, sprawled over his chest. Him, arms lightly wrapped around my naked body, holding me against him.

"I had no idea," I started, licking my dry lips. I really needed to start keeping a big ass bottle of water with me for these kinds of emergencies. "I had no idea it was like that."

The rush of pure, unfiltered desire that came with his bite. I knew vampires liked to fuck—*a lot.* It was practically the only thing they did aside from sleep and feed—or at least as far as I'd seen that was the case. Now I knew why. If they got horny like *that* every time they bit someone...

How could they not?

Frost nodded, his chin rubbing against the top of

ELENA LAWSON

my head. I craned my neck to get a better view of his face. "I didn't know, either, until the first time I fed. It's not like that with blood bags or animals. Only live human or vampire blood causes that reaction.

I pursed my bottom lip. "Vampire blood?" They fed off each other?

Yet another fact I'd neglected to learn.

Frost looked at me strangely. "You know you're a pretty shitty vampire hunter, Rosie. Seems like you don't know your prey at all."

I swatted at him. "Oh, shut up. Why would I care?"

"That sort of information could be useful."

I couldn't think of how, but I didn't bother arguing, waiting for him to answer my question.

"Yes," he breathed, relenting to the prod of my silence. "We can feed from each other. Trading blood is yet another way to stave off the cravings. We can share for a long time, drinking from each other for as long as several weeks without needing even a drop from a bag."

It struck me that he was talking about himself…and the other guys. *We.*

Ethan, Blake, and Frost.

They fed from each other? I thought about them being intimate like that with one another—it was hard to imagine—maybe because I hadn't seen the others in so long it was difficult to picture them. But the warmth flushing my cheeks and the deep squeeze in my belly told me that the idea turned me on a lot more than I thought it would.

For them—for *us*—that sort of thing seemed natural. An eventuality even if they hadn't been turned.

"Wow."

He snorted but made no other comment. "The sun is setting," he added suddenly, and I realized he was right. The barn had darkened, and what remained of the reddish glow of the sun bleeding in through the cracks in the old wood was dying out. I climbed off his chest and ran my hand over the hay looking for my skirt and dug my phone out of the slim pocket when I found it.

"Another eighteen minutes or so and we should be good," I said.

When Frost didn't respond, I spun around to find him staring unblinking at my bare ass.

I snatched up his jeans and threw them at his head playfully, a small part of me inside still shameful for what I felt for him. *You're getting awful chummy with that bloodsucker,* it said, distaste in its tone.

The truth was I'd been helpless to fight it from the very first moment I saw him. This was Frost. And there wasn't any possible way I could have killed him. Or denied what I felt for him. It was there now, stronger than ever, the bond that'd started forming that first day of grade six when he bounded down the walkway of the little brown house next door, backpack slung over one shoulder and a swagger in his step. I'd never forget the first words he said to me after we'd locked eyes at the bus stop near the mouth of the cul-de-sac.

It was the same thing he said to me now, and it melted my heart then as much as it did right now. Tearing down layers of frost and steel I'd worked to build over the last ten years. To protect myself from more heartache.

"You're the most beautiful thing I've ever seen."

*W*e left from Nashville a bit later than planned. The both of us worn out from too many hours spent driving during the night and fucking during the day. I couldn't get enough of him. He refused to bite me again even though, in a moment of fevered desire and weakness, I'd asked him to.

I almost lost control, he told me. *If you hadn't pulled away when you did, I don't know if I could have stopped myself.*

I was at war with myself, too.

My morals and conscience appalled at what I was doing. After so many years spent living in a certain way, the adjustment was going to be difficult. But it was a necessary change if I was going to be able to keep my guys with me this time.

If I rejected them—and their proposal—I had no doubt they would leave me be. If I asked them to go, I knew they would. Though after a few nights spent on the road with Frost and a few more days spent in his bed, with him awakening the parts of me I thought were long dead—I realized leaving them behind was the last thing I wanted.

No matter how wrong a part of me still liked to think all of this was—I couldn't deny there was a *rightness* there, too.

"You're going to chip a tooth doing that," Frost said, and I loosened my grip on the steering wheel, wincing as I leaned back, my muscles tense and sore. I took my foot off the gas for a moment, stretching out my leg—my thigh burning from overuse. I hadn't ever driven as much as I had in the past few weeks.

I'd have a limp by the time we reached Atlanta.

"What?" I asked, confused and coming back to the present.

"That grinding. You've always done that when you're thinking about something real hard."

I made a non-committal sound and shrugged, turning my attention back to the road.

"What are you thinking about?"

"Nothing," I said, maybe a little too quickly. Snapping.

"*Okay,*" he said, elongating the word into several syllables.

It wasn't just the inner turmoil over what was happening between me and Frost that was bothering me. I wondered at how safe they would be if there were actually vampires out there right now—trying to find me. To kill me.

And I worried what Ethan and Blake would think when they saw me.

With my scar and my stakes. Battle hardened and weathered. I wasn't the same as I was.

Sure, Frost had accepted the new me quickly, but that was because, if anything, we were even more alike than we ever were. Bad boy Camden Frost and huntress Rose Ward. We just fit.

But would sweet, smart, and witty Ethan feel the same? Would Blake? He'd always liked my softer parts. Drawn to the girls in class who were quiet and pretty rather than sassy and loud. He respected me—that much I knew. And I was sure he still would. But could Ethan ever feel for me the way Frost did?

I hadn't even seen him yet and I already knew that I *wanted* him to want me that way. I wanted them all to want me that way. I wanted to be like we once were—inseparable friends. Except now that we'd grown—were no longer teenagers—I wanted *more*.

Would they give it to me?

"Don't worry about it," Frost said, reeling me back to the present again.

"Hmm?"

"You have nothing to worry about. They're going to be even happier to see you than you are to see them." Frost rubbed his hands together, a cheeky grin pinning up one corner of his mouth. "I can't wait to see their faces."

I hoped he was right.

We drove on in the moonlight, along a road that grew busier nearer towns and were all but abandoned everywhere else. As though people were afraid to be out in the dark during the witching hours. I pulled up to a gas station about an hour outside of Atlanta—still a few hours until dawn.

Though Frost was now well-fed, and I'd eaten back in St. Louis, I wanted to keep my strength up. I didn't like how weak I'd been when that vampire attacked in my old front yard. Or how weak I'd been after all the adrenaline finally wore off a couple days ago after Frost...

I shivered, the thought igniting a need that slinked down my spine and curled deep in my belly like a sleeping dragon goddess stretching from a long slumber. I couldn't believe I was admitting it—but I *wanted* him to bite me again. And, honestly? I was a bit ticked off that he wouldn't.

The gas station was a 24hr joint, but by the look of the place as we pulled up to one of the pumps, we were the only people here. Inside the fluorescent light lit store within the main building, it didn't even look like there was someone behind the counter.

Annoyingly, though, there were cameras peering down at us from above the pumps—if I left without paying for Bett's fuel, we could have another incident like the one with the cop from a few nights ago.

"I'll gas up," I told Frost. "You go pay."

I'd paid for the last two fuel-ups. The money I'd gotten from the dead vamp in the dumpster was all but gone already. I'd have to get back to work soon, or I'd need to start dipping into my inheritance and I was trying my best to save that. I didn't like spending it.

Having a nice cushion for emergencies made me feel better.

"Oh, and get snacks. And water."

Frost raised a brow at me, but said nothing, slowly pulling on his jacket while I filled up the truck. He stepped out and closed the door behind himself, using both hands to push the white-blond hair from his face and back into place. I marveled at his glutes from the rear, biting my bottom lip as he made his way into the building. Nearly spilling gasoline all over my boots.

"*Fuck,*" I cursed, stepping away from the rapidly growing pool of oily liquid around my feet, figuring that was enough gas anyway. I shoved the nozzle back in and shook my head to clear it, noticing a plaza on the other side of the road.

The windows of all the shops were dark—they'd

long since closed for the night. But smack dab in the middle was a flower shop. I grinned. *Perfect.* I'd wanted to stop in Kansas City to replenish my stock, but we hadn't had enough time. Leaning into the cab, I checked the clock. We had loads of time—and Atlanta was only an hour away.

The three roses I had left in my duffle were falling apart from all the jostling of the truck and wilting from too many days spent not being in the water-filled-vase I always brought with me into motels and the other places I stayed. That wouldn't do. Couldn't have my prey thinking the Black Rose was getting lazy, could we?

I glanced back to find Frost combing the aisles in the store. I still didn't see the shop-keep, but Frost had a reusable black tote in his hand from a rack I saw near the counter and was dutifully filling it with snacks and bottles from the fridges. *Good boy.*

If I was fast, I'd be back before he was able to pay. I tugged off my thin sweater and pulled down the material of my skirt, wondering if I should grab my stakes from the back. I hadn't worn them in a couple days. They'd become something of a pain to keep removing and putting back on and were uncomfortable to sit with between my thighs for long periods.

I'd have bruises there if I hadn't taken them off by now.

Checking to make sure there were no other cars

approaching, I darted across the street and ambled up to the window of the shop. For a small store in the butt-fuck nowhere, it looked to be well stocked and I saw a good number of roses in a small glass temperature-controlled room near the back.

I didn't want to break in—this place was likely someone's livelihood and I wouldn't do that to a human family. But lucky for me most flower shops had *a huge* amount of floral waste. Stems sometimes broke, or the flowers were just a little *too* bloomed. People generally wanted the kind that were still just starting to bud so they could be admired longer.

I was no exception—but I wouldn't be picky. There weren't all that many flower shops open twenty-four hours and a girl had to sleep. On flower days, I'd have to stay up an extra two or three hours to make it to one for opening time.

The building was long and thin, with small laneways on either side leading around back. That was where I'd find them. Looking over my shoulder, I saw a flicker of movement inside the store. Good, Frost was still inside.

Didn't need him flipping out when he returned to the truck to see I'd gone.

My boots hit the concrete with muted thuds as I quietly ran around back, keeping an ear on my surroundings. There may not be vamps out here, but there could still be animals. And humans can be just as dangerous.

Guns are just as deadly as fangs.

When I rounded the corner of the brick wall, I saw a few petals scattered on the ground. Oddly enough, they were rose petals. After a cursory glance up, I saw a barren laneway, short fat green bits outside of steel gray doors lining all the way from one end of the building to the other.

And the petals, red as crimson in the moonlight, were scattered in a near-perfect trail all the way to the bin at the middle of the building. My blood flooded with energy at the same moment my sixth sense picked up on the change in the atmosphere.

Being with Frost for so many days, I'd grown accustomed to the feeling and almost hadn't noticed it. But there it was in full force again, and somehow, I knew it wasn't Frost.

No. This was someone else. Another vampire. And judging by the strength of the feeling—the itching like ants crawling over the surface of my skin—the roiling in my gut and sharpness of my focus—it was an older vampire.

The feeling was stronger when they were stronger.

Fuck.

I'd left my stakes in the car.

Where are you, fucker? Come out.

I felt the prickle of his eyes on me a second later but

didn't dare look up. He was on top of the building—probably thought this was the perfect trap for the Black Rose. A trail of the petals I was named for leading right to my prize. He probably thought he was so clever.

And maybe he was.

I was still going to kill him. I'd do it with my bare hands if I had to.

But wait…the glint of something metal poked out from underneath the flower bin. *Please be a crowbar. Please be a crowbar.*

I quieted my pulse, stooping low to lift a petal as though I'd only just noticed they were there. He had gravity on his side—if I ran, he would beat me to the dumpster. I'd have to play this cool and hope he would wait until I was right underneath him to attack.

With a steady pace, I moved, my boots grinding petals underfoot. I didn't dare look up. Did my best to sooth the rush of adrenaline trying to coerce my heart into a canter the vamp would likely be able to hear.

Where are you, Frost?

This was his fault. If it weren't for him, I'd have my stakes strapped to my thighs right now—or I'd at least have brought them with me. He was distracting me. Making my stakes less convenient to have between my legs when his cock kept finding its way there.

Godfuckingdamnit.

Swallowing, the muscles in my arms flexed and the

tendons in my back pulled taut, forcing my spine erect as I reached out for the lid of the bin, planning to drop low and grab whatever makeshift weapon was beneath the bin before he could drop in on me.

I blew out a breath and my hand closed over the bin. I wrenched the lid up and dropped to the ground, yanking out the bit of metal at the same moment I heard the telltale *thud* of a vampire landing only a few yards away. I straightened my spine, wielding the slim bit of curved metal in my palm.

The vampire sneered, the glint of laughter in his dark eyes.

In my hand was a rusted silver spoon. The kind they used for soup at greasy diners. Still caked with a bit of browned cream if I wasn't mistaken.

Oh fuck.

I gritted my teeth, wanting to laugh, too. How much more ridiculous could this get.

Ugh.

I chanced another glance at the vamp, finding him to be cool and collected. Paler than most. With eyes that spoke of an age far beyond my years. He was *old.* And old meant powerful.

There was a good chance this one's compulsion would be stronger than mine—so that tactic was out, too.

"What's the matter, pet," the vampire crooned, taking a step nearer as I discarded the spoon—preferring the sharpness of my claws. "You seem surprised to see me."

He stepped in and I stepped back, it was a dangerous dance, neither one of us closing the gap, but unable to move more than the seven feet of space between us. He could close the distance in a fraction of a second when he decided to, I'd have to be ready.

If only I could get him all the way to the edge of the building, I might be able to get Frost's attention, but I doubted he'd let me go so far.

"The Black Rose, I presume?" he purred, and I saw in his expression a prideful gleam. *He thinks he's done it. That it's over.*

He obviously didn't know who or what he was up against. The Black Rose wasn't about to go down without a good cat fight. And kitty's got claws.

I pouted my bottom lip, giving him a nod. "And you must be Vlad. A Pleasure. But if you don't mind—I've got to be going. You know, vampires to kill and whatnot."

The vampire shook his head incredulously, still advancing forward, backing me closer and closer to the laneway that could save me. "How?" he asked.

I knew what he meant right away. It was what Frost was wondering, too, I was sure. How did a human girl take down a vampire? And not just one—the number had risen close to triple digits now, if it hadn't already surpassed that. I was a serial killer, but I didn't think the local authorities would arrest me if they knew who —*no*—*what* I was killing. They'd thank me. If they believed me.

I preferred the term vigilante. It had a nicer ring to it.

The vamp had stopped walking and there were still several meters to go before I would be out in the open. I could see from the change in his stance that he meant to attack…any second now. I'd run out of time. *Fuck.*

"Like this," I hissed and launched myself at him with everything I had.

The vampire was faster, he parried my advance, and, in a blur, I watched, unable to stop him as he drove the heel of his hand into my chest. The air rushed from my body and I flew, sailing through the air, choking, *gasping,* until my back smashed against brick, closely followed by the back of my head.

The brick cracked and crumbled, buckling at the force of my impact.

I crumpled to the ground. Dazed, still struggling for air, spots of light and darkness gyrating in my line of sight, making everything hazy and unfocused. So, I didn't see him when he stepped in, his cold hand closing around my throat, lifting me up—pressing me back.

He squeezed, but not so much that I had no airflow, just enough to hold me there. Why wasn't he ending it? It didn't matter. I still had time.

I'm still alive.

I could still fight him. My vision came back in specks first and then blotches and then a few more blinks and I was staring into the eyes of the predator. The blue eyes. *Damn.* Not the right one.

My feet dangled in the air, and I feigned weakness as he leaned in. I thought he was going to bite me, and my body tensed, ready to kick out at him. Trying to discern where his dick was beneath his long coat. Not even a vampire was impervious to a good kick in the nuts.

"*You're* the Black Rose?" he spat. "And he said I'd have trouble bringing you in…how pathetic."

I saw red.

He drew back and I knew if I looked into his eyes, he'd have me. He was older and stronger. He would compel me to go with him. Or to sit idly while he bled me dry and there would be nothing, I could do about it. I had to do something *now* before it was too late.

Hauling in as much air as I could with his hand clamped around my neck, I used the wall as a springboard against my back and heel kicked him in the middle with both heeled feet. His hand roughly broke from my neck and it seemed I'd landed at least one good blow to his nether regions because the poor sap hunched over, a choked noise coming from his throat. Blood soaked his hand from where the five-inch heels had punctured his abdomen—and hopefully—his dick, too.

Now who's pathetic?

My advantage wouldn't last long, and though the daze from being tossed into a *motherfucking brick wall* hadn't totally subsided, I was coherent enough to know that and act on it.

A glimmer of silver in the light snagged my eye and I saw the spoon I'd discarded a few feet away and smiled. A weapon was a weapon. This time I wouldn't be picky. The vampire made an attempt to stand, half-assed if you asked me, but I'd already gotten the spoon and I didn't hesitate this time. When he opened his mouth in a feral snarl and launched for the attack, I used his own momentum against him with a well-placed greasy ass silver dining utensil.

It plunged into his eye socket, stunning him while I twirled around his prone form and drove the heel of my boot into his back—six ribs up—a little to the left. It was no metal stake or Katana, but it would have to do.

I wasn't fully confident in the placement of my blow until he fell to his knees, gurgling his last breaths. The heel broke off with the pull of his fall and my foot landed back on the gravel, the boot ruined, leaving me with a duck-footed walk as I limped, one leg higher up than the other to the bastard.

"I'm sorry," I said, a bit breathless—more from the high than the blow he delivered now. "What was that you were saying?" I taunted, relishing in how he paled. How blood leaked in a steady stream from his mouth. "Something about me being…pathetic, was it?"

Motherfucker.

"Here," I said, tearing the heel from my other boot. I knelt down and rammed it into his chest, hearing the one I'd hit him with from the back clatter to the ground. He sputtered, his clawed hands trying to reach for me—to fight. His spooned eye looked gruesome and dark with clotted blood. Nasty. "You might as well have the other one," I snapped. "*Pathetic?* Fucking dick."

With a furious heat sizzling down my back, I hobbled over to the dumpster in the middle of the building on my fucked-up shoes. I probably looked like a damned deranged duck. I tore open the lid, the tiny metal lock holding it shut snapped off with a small *chink* and scattered to the ground.

Inside the bin were lilies, azaleas, some other colorful shit I didn't know the name of and *ah...yes.* Roses. I grabbed a few and threw one in the general direction of the vampire. "There," I called out to him. "A souvenir!"

He fell onto his face, landing with his one still functional eye almost perpendicular to the flower. Good, let that be the last thing he sees.

I left him there to die slow, hobbling on my duck feet out to the side of the building and around to the front, where a few cars passed by—the first I'd heard since going around the plaza. Of course, *now* there were people. If I'd heard cars, I might have tried to make a break for it.

And where the *fuck* was Frost?

Across the street, I found him, his silver head bobbing this way and that as he exited the gas station, a bulging black bag in one hand and a Slurpee in the other.

His eyes met mine from across the street and he hollered. "Hey! What are you doing? We gotta move, Ward!"

I shook my head and ambled across the highway. Once I was in the light and he was able to fully take me in, he paled, his eye widening. His mouth dropped open, speechless. I snatched the Slurpee right out of his hand, taking a long pull of Sprite flavored ice. My favorite.

He was lucky.

I winced, recoiling when he touched the tender spot on my head—his fingertips coming away wet with sticky blood. "The fuck…?"

"A little help might be nice next time," I said, "But thanks for doing the shopping, honey." I patted him on the chest with the hand that was still full of thorny roses as I turned to hop back into the truck.

13

"*A* spoon?" he asked incredulously as he lumbered back into the Betty's cab five minutes later. He'd zipped across the highway and behind the building, not believing me when I told him I'd had to use my heels and a spoon because I neglected to put on my stakes.

A mistake I wouldn't soon repeat. They were now securely strapped to my thighs and I wouldn't be taking them off ever again. Maybe not even in the shower. Maybe not even during sex.

"How the hell did you manage that?"

I shrugged, polishing off the Slurpee as I started the truck, swaying a little to the left. My body worked hard to heal the wound to my head, but it throbbed now that the adrenaline had worn off and the dizziness seemed like it was only getting worse. The pain in my back was awful, too, but at least that was bearable.

And the Slurpee had numbed the burning in my throat. *Thank you, Frost!*

"I just…" I trailed off. Wait, what was I saying?

Something about a soup? No. A spoon.

When I blinked, the darkness tried to stick. Made my eyelids and limbs heavy. A cool sweat coated my chest and I heard a miniscule sound. Like a moan, or a whine.

My blood rushed to my head and I gasped—the pain a searing knife of heat lancing through my skull.

"Christ!" I heard the curse only a few seconds before the darkness latched on—holding tight and not letting go. The last thing I felt as the pressure in my skull rose to a deafening crescendo were strong arms and soft leather on my cheek.

14

"Are you sure she's going to be alright?" A honeyed voice asked, the cadence succinct, if a little strained.

"I checked her head wound," replied another male voice—this one smoky and gruff. "She's already started to heal. She should be alright within a few hours if she keeps healing at this rate."

"You don't think we need to call a doctor, then?" This one I knew, it was Frost.

I heard movement outside wherever I was and then the one with the smoky voice replied to Frost. "No. I don't understand how—but she seems to be healing at ten times the rate of a normal human—maybe even a bit faster than that."

I stretched out carefully, feeling around myself in the dark, working out the kinks in my bones. Glad

when I found none were broken. The business of reset-
ting partially healed bones wasn't my favorite. I was
glad I wouldn't have to ask Frost to help me out with
setting them.

But where the hell were we?

The smooth silk under my calloused palms was
warm, so I knew we'd been here a while—wherever
here was. It was almost pitch dark and I had to squint
into the dim to make out the shape of a chair against
the far wall and the boxy outline of a nightstand and
lamp next to the bed. The smells of juniper and
patchouli and spice assaulted my nose and it wrinkled
at the smell.

Pot-pourri. God, I hated the smell of pot-pourri.

A hotel then?

Slowly, I moved to the edge of the bed where I'd
been put—noticing how everything except for my
panties had been removed.

My mind whirred with worry at that for a moment
before I realized Frost would have wanted to check my
whole body over for injury. He was thorough. Always
had been. I sat up and my head throbbed painfully. Not
nearly as bad as it'd been before, but still sore.

I sucked a breath in through my teeth.

Fuck. And still tender to the touch.

Ow.

Obviously, the vampire had done some damage. I
should have been healed by now. The fucker must have

cracked my skull. Not the first time it'd happened, but as I stood on shaking legs, wincing, I made myself a promise that it would be the last.

The low hum of conversation outside the cracked open door continued, but they must have moved further away—or the throbbing in my head had procured a voice box and was drowning out the sound of them. The pulsating throbs audible with each beat of my heart.

I saw a glass of water on the nightstand and snatched it with greedy, shaking fingers. Like a dehydrated fish, I dumped it down my throat, reveling in how it rid me of the awful dryness and putrid taste in my mouth. The throbbing spiked and then subsided after a few long breaths.

Food.

I needed food if I was going to be able to heal the rest of this wound. Healing took energy, just like it did for vampires. Except where they needed blood, I needed Cheetos and a few bags of the barbeque peanuts I saw in the sack of goodies Frost had procured from the gas station. And maybe a Gatorade.

Sugar helped. So did electrolytes. I fumbled around in the dark, trying to find where he put my clothes, but having no luck. And after feeling all along the walls, I found no light switch, either.

Ah, fuck it. I'd never been shy—I didn't care who the people were Frost was talking to, I wanted my damned clothes back. *Now.* Besides, one of them said they 'checked me' already, so I was sure he'd gotten an eyeful.

I reefed the door open and stepped out into the dimly lit hall, following the voices down and to the right, where light was pouring into the darkened hallway. My fists were clenched as I turned the corner.

"Frost," I growled. "Where the hell are my—"

I stopped short; three sets of eyes turned at my approach. Eyes I knew well. Suddenly being almost fully naked didn't seem like a good idea. I itched to cover myself, but that would only make it more awkward, so instead I placed my hands firmly on my hips and heaved in a breath, trying to draw some extra confidence in with it.

"Look what the cat dragged in," Blake said before I could formulate words. His gray eyes roamed my curves with practiced restraint, devouring me inch by inch. That burning sensation in the back of my throat had returned, warning me that tears were not far behind.

No. I wouldn't cry.

I'm not going to cry.

"Rose," Ethan said, the tops of his ears pink, his steeped tea eyes flitting low before he managed to drag them back to my face. I thought he was staring at my breasts but realized with a jolt and a sinking feeling that he was actually looking at my scar.

I'd never seen him with short hair, but it suited him. The honey blonde color was the same, though, and it still curled up in the front, even though it was only three inches long on the top. "How are you feeling? Do you have any dizziness? Nausea?"

I grinned at him. He was always our mother hen. Making sure the rest of us had what we needed. He'd been the one to hold my hair back the first time I drank...and ended up hugging the porcelain goddess for hours afterward. Fireball and I still didn't agree to this day.

Frost nodded to me, acknowledging the emotions I was sure he could see clear as day written all over my face.

"Come here," I croaked. "Both of you." But I was already going to them, almost tripping in my haste to get past the armchairs and thick carpet in the living area to where they were all standing around a narrow section of bar jutting out from the kitchen in the condo-like space.

Blake was the first to move in, eagerly taking me into his arms, my hardened breasts pressing against the soft material of his clean black suit jacket. He looked so different, and then yet so much the same, too. With dark brown hair that bordered on being black and those gray eyes set into a face that would make angels jealous. With those cheekbones and that dimple in his chin. The sharp line of his freshly shaven jaw. I could feel the muscle rippling beneath my embrace. Could see the start of coiling black tattoos peaking up from his collar and jutting out from his jacket cuffs.

Damn, he looked good. Almost too good. He'd always been the prettiest of us all, but after ten years I could see that age had defined him. Turned the boyish handsomeness into a sexy manliness that had my inner lioness roaring to explore what lay beneath his clothes.

I squeezed him tightly and buried my face into his neck. He flinched at the contact of skin on skin and I worried I'd overstepped, I loosed my hold on him and tipped my head back to gauge his reaction.

Blake pulled away, unapologetic as he took his bottom lip between his teeth and breathed low and heavy, glaring down at the curve of my breasts. "Damn, Rose. You're…"

"Not a kid anymore?"

"Definitely not."

"Neither are you."

Ethan appeared beside Blake with a fluffy white bathrobe in his hands. Always the gentleman. His ears were still pink, and his mouth was set in a way that told me he was doing his best not to show just how much my nakedness was affecting him. He helped me into the robe and the instant I was done belting it in the middle, he tugged me into a hug.

Where Blake and Frost were practically giants compared to my small frame, I fit more snuggly in the arms of Ethan. He wasn't short by any means, but he was close enough to my size that my face fit perfectly into the crook of his neck. I breathed in his scent, finding that he still used the same cologne he did as a teenager. The nautical scent of it mixed with his own natural musk in a way that made me sigh, wanting to drink him in.

I could have stayed like that forever.

And then I remembered why I was here. And why the back of my neck was prickling with unease even though I should have been more comfortable than I had in ages. They were my guys. My best friends.

But now…they weren't human anymore.

I pulled away from Ethan, but held him close, searching his soft brown eyes for the *him* I remembered. He smiled and the dimples in his cheeks deepened. The skin around his eyes crinkled. Like Frost, I could see Ethan was still in there, too.

Being changed hadn't taken away their humanity— or at least, not all of it.

The revelation left me relieved, but also with a sour taste in my mouth. I didn't want to question all the vampire lives I'd taken. I didn't want to think that there was a chance some of them hadn't deserved it.

Because then…what would that make *me*?

"You gave us a pretty good scare there, Rosie," Frost said from where he stood on the other side of the counter, his arms crossed over his chest as he leaned against the high bar counter, a half-full glass of whisky to his left.

"You worry too much. I wouldn't have survived this long doing what I do if I was weak."

The three guys shared a look. "Rose…" Ethan trailed off. "That head injury should have killed you, or at least…left you hospitalized."

"When we figured out the Black Rose was you, we thought—well, we thought you'd done what we had." Blake added in his smoky voice, the low pitch of it made my knees quake. *Fuck,* what were these guys doing to me?

I bit the inside of my cheek and tucked my hands deep into the soft pockets of the robe to keep my mind on more important things. "Wait," I said, my throbbing brain catching up to his meaning all at once. "You thought I *turned* myself?"

Frost took a swallow of his whiskey and set the glass down. "What else were we supposed to think, Rose? A human couldn't have killed the number of vampires you did?"

"It's impossible," Ethan agreed, backing up to sit on one of the stools against the counter.

I hated how they were all looking at me—waiting for an explanation I didn't have. It was an explanation I both longed for and never *ever* wanted to hear. Not sure I could handle knowing the truth of why I was like this. Why I had a muted version of a vampire's strength and heightened senses. Why I could compel and move faster than the fastest human on the planet. Why I could out-lift the boys in high school and always won first place in track—by *a lot.*

"Stop looking at me like that," I snapped, unable to handle it anymore. *"I don't know, okay,"* I hissed, answering their unasked question. "I don't know why I'm like this. I don't know *what I am.* I've never known." And then, deciding to give them more than I'd ever admitted to anyone else before, I added, "My mom was like this, too. It's what got her killed."

When the vampire first approached us, he'd said something I wouldn't ever forget. *Don't you remember me?* And when she didn't answer, gathering me into her arms to shove me behind her, to use her own body as a shield to protect me, he'd laughed. *You, a* human, *made me leave. Told me to never return to Washington. I still can't step foot over the state line, you know, and I won't be able to until you're dead.*

She'd made a mistake. The first lesson I ever learned about compulsion I learned that night, because since we didn't live in Seattle anymore, he was able to find her. We no longer lived within the state line she compelled him out of.

He could find her because she didn't make him forget her. She told him to leave and never come back, but she left him with the memory of her face.

And she died for it.

"So, it's genetic?" Ethan asked, his gaze growing distant. I could see the gears and cogs turning in his mind, trying to figure it out. He was always the smartest of us. A slender finger of hope trailed over the fist of dread in my chest. If anyone could figure out what I was, he could.

"Whatever *it* is…yeah. It must be."

"Did you ever," Blake asked, and I wondered if he was thinking about our first and only kiss. It was the first place my mind went. "Compel *us?*"

I shook my head. "I don't think so," I said honestly. "If I ever did, it wasn't on purpose."

Blake pursed his lips and nodded, accepting of my reply. Lost in thought.

It was surreal being here. In this weird condo with the blackout curtains along the far wall closed tight to seal out the light. Surrounded by the childhood friends I'd longed to see for ten years—but who I thought had no interest in seeing me. How wrong I'd been…

It made my heart expand, straining to remain in its shriveled state. They were still together after all this time—and now we were a foursome again. I swallowed and gratefully accepted the plate Frost pulled out of the refrigerator in the kitchen opposite the counter and slid over to me. A steak salad was covered tightly with a film of plastic wrap. It looked absolutely divine. I recognized the green sauce on top to be chimichurri. Ethan's mom used to make it all the time.

I eyed him as I unwrapped the cling film and took Frost's proffered fork. "Thank you," I said to Ethan, knowing it was him who'd done the cooking.

He nodded.

"So, where are we exactly?"

"Atlanta," came Ethan's gruff reply.

"I gathered that," I said rather sardonically. We'd been headed there, only an hour or so away—maybe even less—when we stopped at the gas station. And by the look of the knit sweater draped over the back of the sofa in the adjoining living area and the shoes by the door. A book that had to be Ethan's on the coffee table. They'd been here a while.

Ethan came to lean on the counter across from me, next to Frost as I took the first savory mouthful of chimichurri steak and fresh garden lettuce, moaning at how good it tasted. "It's a rental," Ethan said. "A temporary living space while we tried to find you."

"Well," I said, mouth still half-full of steak. "You found me."

Ethan's face cracked into a smile and I couldn't help but return it. Those dimples got me every time and it seemed it didn't matter how long it'd been; they still had the same effect. "Where do you all live," I asked. "You know—like, normally."

Blake yanked out the barstool next to me and swiveled it around until it was inches away, hopping on top and leaning into my side. "We could tell you, but then we'd have to kill you," he joked, but there was an edge of malice to his voice, and his warm breath against the base of my neck made my stomach clench and my spine tingle.

I was in *big* trouble with these three.

Now that I'd been with one vampire—a thing I never would have dreamed of doing in my wildest fantasies—being with two others seemed only natural. Especially since they were the other two of a foursome that was almost fifteen years in the making.

"Ethan?" I hedged, crooking my brow at him. Knowing he would be the one to give me answers.

"Baton Rouge."

"Ethan!" Both Frost and Blake said at the same time.

"What?" Ethan chided, but I didn't miss the small recoil of his face from Frost's clenched fists. "It's *Rose*," he said like it was the simplest thing in the world. "It's not like we hadn't already planned on taking her there, anyway."

"She hasn't agreed yet," Frost growled back at Ethan.

Blake shoved him. "You pretty much just gave a professional vampire killer our home address."

Hardly, I thought, but remained quiet while they sorted it out, savoring every morsel of the meal in front of me.

The three of them grimaced at one another, practically snarling. I shook my head and rolled my eyes.

Boys... "If I was going to kill you, I'd have done it already," I said between mouthfuls.

Ethan's lips parted and his eyes widened in surprise at my words. A crease formed in his brow.

"I was *joking*," I said, trying to erase the worry tainting his handsome face. "Well, I mean, I wasn't joking—I would have killed you already if that was my intent, but it's not my intent. I couldn't ever hurt you —*any* of you. So just relax," I rambled off, stuffing another forkful of tender steak in my mouth.

Ethan looked between Frost and I. "Has Frost even asked you yet?"

I swallowed, feeling the throbbing subside even more before I answered him. "What? About this *proposition* he keeps talking about?"

No one answered.

"No," I said. "I wanted to wait until we got here, so I could see you all before I made any sort of decision."

Blake smiled mischievously, his grin making my toes curl. "Good," he said and wrapped an arm possessively around my waist making my stomach do a little flip. I remembered him being like this with other girls. A bit controlling even as a teenager. Liking them to *submit*, I thought. He obviously hadn't changed in that regard, but this was the first time he'd set his sights on me as a target.

I smiled at Blake sheepishly. "Cocky as ever," I said, a little breathless.

"Hey, it's only fair," he said, and I saw his eyes flicker to Frost and back to me.

I chucked a piece of steak at Frost. "You *told* them?"

I couldn't believe the bastard told them we'd fucked. I mean, there had never been secrets between us, but he should have at least asked me first, *the prick*.

Frost tossed the steak back on my plate and smirked. "You'll be wanting to eat that."

He was right, of course, and I stabbed it with my fork and popped it into my mouth. "Don't think just because I slipped up a bit—"

"*A lot,*" Frost corrected with a glint in his eye.

I grimaced.

"*Relax,*" Blake said. "I won't bite unless you ask me too."

Gulp.

Trying to rein the conversation back in, I flipped back to the reason I was even here. "So, this proposition," I said, glancing from Frost to Ethan—avoiding Blake entirely. "What is it?"

"We want you to be our blood mate," Blake rasped in my ear.

"Your *what?*"

15

I stood from the bar table, the chair dragging back loudly against the tile with a metallic screech. "You don't mean..." I trailed off, unable to wipe the bitter look from my face or take the saltiness out of my voice.

"Yes," Ethan said, looking subdued and more than a little sorry—his jaw twitching. "For lack of a better way to explain it—we want you to be our vampire bride."

Holy fucking shit.

I opened my mouth only to shut it again, so many words at the tip of my tongue vying to be said that I just stammered and stumbled, making undiscernible sounds. Sputtering.

How dare they ask that?

What the hell were they playing at?

They were idiots if they thought that I would actually…

I saw the hurt in Ethan's eyes as he forced himself to look away. I saw the betrayal in Blake's. But Frost remained cool as he rose to his full height. "She's human," he said, his tone unapproachable. "That changes things."

Right. I forgot they thought I was already a vampire, and that that was how I was able to hunt them as well as I did. If I *was* a vampire—*which I most certainly am not*—then their request wouldn't seem so out of left field.

"So, you won't do it, then?" Blake asked, that maniacal glimmer back in his eyes. When I didn't answer right away, he stood, his stare turning haughty and accusing. "It's a simple yes or no question, Rose."

"No," I breathed, unable to force myself to even consider it. "I'm sorry—I won't."

They were *asking me to* turn. Did they themselves not regret it? How could they ask that of me? Of anyone? To discard their soul without a care and trade in *life* for an eternity of dark.

Any bit of emotion that was on Ethan's face vanished. His expression went utterly blank as he turned from the countertop and strode from the room.

"Ethan," I called after him, watching him grab the knit sweater from the back of the sofa as he went down the hallway. He didn't turn around, not even after I called his name a second time.

"Give him time to process," Frost said without any worry or inflection in his voice. "You know how he is."

I did. I knew how they all were, and yet...I'd never expected this.

Fuck, if they'd asked me to be their *human* bride, I may have considered it. After getting reacquainted with them, it would probably be the only thing I wanted. To be with them. I could still picture it—even knowing it was impossible.

The images hurt more than I cared to admit.

I understood their request well enough—or as well as I could. I knew little of the intricacies of vampire life, mostly because I spent so much time *ending* it. But I knew that female vampires were rare. They tended to die during the transformation or if not then shortly after. It was said to be excruciating.

Because the females were so rare, the males who preferred the company of females usually formed a sort of protective group around them. Effectively making the female their *queen* of sorts. She holds the power because she could easily leave her blood mates and go find another group. They kill for her. They do her bidding. They protect her.

It was why out of all the vampires I'd killed—the number close to the hundred mark—I'd only ever encountered three females. Two were freshly changed and barely knew what was happening to them. The other was a blood mate—and I killed her entire clan that night.

Why they wanted *me* to be theirs was beyond my comprehension to understand. *Hell,* why they wanted *any* female vampire to hold sway over them was beyond me. Why not just live rogue like so many other vampires? Frost said they were intimate with each other, so then why did they even need a female? There was obviously something more to it than I knew.

"You don't have to make a decision now," Frost said.

I opened my mouth to object. I wanted to tell him that I would never agree. I didn't want any of them thinking it could be a possible eventuality. But he stopped me with a raised hand and stern look.

"We may need to rethink things, too," he said, eyeing Blake who had stolen Frost's whiskey and was now draining the glass dry, clearly pissed. "I've taken her blood," Frost told Blake, and I realized he hadn't shared that part of our intimacy until now.

Blake gaped at Frost. Was that jealousy I saw in his eyes?

"She was able to replenish it within minutes, maybe even faster than that. And so long as she's well-fed and hydrated, we know she heals other wounds fairly quick, too. She's strong and fast. Her senses must be nearly to the level of ours..." he trailed off, letting Blake fill in blanks.

Blake nodded as though understanding what Frost was getting at.

I, on the other, hand, wasn't getting it. I was hopelessly lost. "I'm sorry," I said. "What are you two talking about? I'm not following."

Frost looked at me apologetically. "Rosie, other than having sharp teeth and the need for blood, you might as well be one already."

I choked trying to formulate a response. "*No. That's not true.*"

Blake sighed. "Afraid it is, love. Frost is right. Those are all vampire traits."

"That isn't the only thing," Frost added. "I almost couldn't control the urge to drain her." From the way he said it, as though surprised, I got the sense that he wasn't joking about teaching himself rigid control. "And after I fed from her, I…" he trailed off, and I scrunched my brows, trying to read his awestruck expression.

"You what, Frost?" Blake asked, peering between the two of us like I had any idea what the hell he was talking about.

Frost's river-green eyes flitted up to meet mine, and then Blakes. "I've *never* felt stronger. I haven't had even a lick of thirst since, either."

Blake seemed to be mulling over what he said, but I wasn't really paying attention to them anymore. I was thinking that it was just my fucking luck that *my* blood would be like some supernatural battery acid for them. Of course, it was. Until Frost bit me the other night, no other fangs had ever pierced my flesh. There were close calls, but I'd never been bitten until Frost.

"Do you think that's why Rafe…?" Blake asked Frost in a voice filled with quiet rage.

Rafe? Was Rafe the same as the Raphael Frost had mentioned a few nights back?

"Who are you talking about?"

Neither answered. Their mouths shutting with near audible sounds.

I glanced between them. Why weren't they answering me?

Fed up, I shoved my plate away and stood, pulling my robe tighter around myself. "I need a shower," I announced. "And when I come back out, you better be ready to tell me exactly what it is I'm missing because *clearly* there's more you aren't telling me."

I left them to sit stunned at the countertop as I made for the entrance to the hallway across the room. "And save me some *goddamn* whiskey," I hollered back at the sound of a screw cap being lifted from a glass bottle.

I was going to need it.

16

The blood, dirt, and grime of the last twenty-four hours ran from my skin as scalding water cascaded over me. the droplets of pink and varying shades of brown and gray mingled along their path down my body, creating a morbid work of art before they were swirled away. Swallowed up by the metal maw of the shower drain. I sighed at the warmth —and the sense of being totally *clean* that I hadn't had in weeks.

Hell, after a motel shower sometimes I felt I was even more dirty.

But this? This was fucking bliss. The bathroom I found a couple doors down from my bedroom was fit for a queen. With pyramids of plush white towels and fancy soaps. Marble floors and countertops. Gold faucets and drawer handles. A claw-footed soaker tub that I had been tempted to bathe in but thought better of it. I was far too dirty for a bath. Instead I decided the glass box at the edge of the room looked just as tempting with its rain-head shower jutting out the top, and the steam settings on a panel on the wall inside.

I was right. It was glorious. I took my time, wondering how long it would be before all the hot water was gone. I'd wager it'd have taken all day, judging by the layout of the condo and the wide covered windows —it was a big building. I could have stayed in there for hours, but after only about thirty minutes there was a knock at the door, and I figured I should hurry up.

It might've been the only bathroom in the building. Vamps didn't need to go as much as humans, hardly at all, but they did still function in those regions.

"I'll be right out," I hollered, a little more acid in my voice than I intended. They better have a glass of whiskey ready for me...

The frigid air outside the door after the steamy heat of the fancy ass shower made me shiver as I tip toed across the cool tile to grab a towel, leaving little wet footprints against the black-and-white checkered floor.

I tugged the towel around me and used a second one to dry my hair as best I could as I made my way back over to the door, careful to avoid the slippery pools of water I'd created all over the place.

I opened the door and a billowing cloud of steam

exited with me, evaporating in the empty hallway. *Fuck*, and I thought it was cold in the bathroom? It was freezing out here. I pulled the towel tighter around myself, shivering as my body adjusted to the massive temperature difference.

Who the hell was knocking?

I listened for noise but couldn't hear much of anything. My ears still filled with the whirring sound of the exhaust fan in the bathroom.

"Hey."

My elbow connected with taut tissue and bone and there was a grunt and a stomp before I realized I elbowed Frost in the chest. His jaw clenched as he rose from his hunched position to his full height, his eyes and forehead straining with the effort of trying to hide his obvious pain and discomfort. He looked constipated. I almost laughed.

"You really shouldn't sneak up on people like that," I said with a smile in my voice, barely contained laughter bubbling to the surface.

"Noted," he replied, his voice breathy and tight.

I snorted.

Wincing, Frost jerked his head down the hallway, toward a door that was standing open close to the end. It was the room I'd woken up in, or at least, I thought it was. There were so many doors in this place. The door was cracked open, and it seemed someone had found the light switch after all. A warm ivory glow poured out onto the hardwood.

"The sun set about a half hour ago," Frost said, and I stared at him agape. How long had I been out? It wasn't even sunrise when I passed out the day before. "Ethan went and got your duffle for you. It's in the room there so you can change."

"And then we'll talk?" I asked, giving him a hard look. I needed more answers. The dots were starting to connect themselves in my head, or trying to, but it was hard to connect dots when half the ones you needed to form the picture were missing entirely.

Frost nodded solemnly. "And then we'll talk."

I nodded and couldn't help myself as I leaned up on tip toe and kissed him on the cheek. The skin was smooth—velvety. He must've had time to shave since we arrived here. "Thank you," I told him. "For bringing me here."

And for so much more I can't find the words to say.

I hoped he knew how much all of this meant to me. I'd never been good at talking about this sort of thing. My half-assed thank-you was all he would get. But this was Frost. I'd be lucky to get half as much from him if the situation were reversed.

"Welcome," he said low and throaty, making my throat dry and my pulse pick up.

How the *hell* did he have that effect on me?

Before I could decide to jump him right there in the

hallway, I blinked away the haze of desire, shook my head, and hurried in the opposite direction down the hall and into the room near the end, closing the door behind me.

I leaned my head against it, breathing heavy, my palm pressed flat against the woodgrain. *Get a grip, Rose!* I told myself. How was I supposed to make any sort of rational decision when—

"Found this in your bag," a smoky voice said from behind me, the low cadence slinking across the small space, making my stomach muscles tighten.

I whirled around, clenching the towel to myself, sending a spray of water against the wall from my long hair as it whipped out around me.

"Wow," Blake said, raising a hand from the bowl-like armchair he was slouched in. "It's just me." He wiped a few small drops of water from his face where I splashed him, his eyes hot and hungry. *Oh shit.* "I'm supposed to be the one getting *you* all wet," he purred.

Oh no he didn't.

"What are you—" I started, but then I noticed what he was holding in his other hand. The long, thick, veiny piece of deep purple silicone. "Mr. Dickins!" I exclaimed, rushing over to snatch him back from the clutches of his captor.

"Mr. Dickins?" Blake asked, a rare smile lighting up his face. "Really, Rose? You named your vibrator?"

He held it up and out of my reach, back behind his

head so I would have to practically lay across him to get it. I knew what he was playing at. I stopped just shy of crawling onto his lap. "Give. Him. Back."

"Oh, so it's a *him* now, is it?"

What was he trying to do? Hadn't he been pissed at me before I left to get into the shower? Now he was… what? Taunting me? *Teasing* me?

Bastard.

Well two could play at that game. "What? Jealous, Blake?" I asked, a hand on my toweled hip. "Is my Mr. Dickins making you feel insecure?"

By all rights, Mr. Dickins wasn't huge. A respectable six inches. But from the shit lays I'd had before Frost, I knew finding one over five inches could be difficult. I mean, sure, size isn't everything.

In fact, five inches could be perfect if used effectively. But most had *no idea* how to please a woman.

Blake's eyes widened infinitesimally before he tossed Mr. Dickins on the bed—my chargeable boyfriend forgotten for the moment. "I should spank you for that," he growled, and I saw a flash of real fury in his gaze, mingling with something more like lust.

Oh.

I resisted the urge to tell him to go right ahead. *Rose could use a good spanking.*

I'd always wondered how Blake's particular brand of romance would shape him as an adult. Now I got the feeling I knew. And suddenly this all made sense. This was his apology. Like me, Blake wasn't good at *those* kinds of words. But I bet I knew what he *was* good at...

I cleared my throat, my face warming. *Fuck, did someone turn up the heat in this place? Wasn't I freezing like two seconds ago?*

"Didn't your—um—mother ever tell you it's rude to... to go through a woman's things?" I stuttered, stepping back a foot or two away from him so I could catch my breath.

My eyes roved over his black suit jacket, admiring how it was tight in the crease of his elbows, the buttons undone to show a tapered middle in a thin white t-shirt. Black ink peeking out from his cuffs and covering the tiny bit of smooth flesh where his t-shirt was riding up, showing that deeply dipping V that disappeared below his waistline.

When I looked up, he was smirking at me, pleased with my reaction to him. His dark obsidian eyes glinting in the light of the canvas covered lamp hanging a few paces behind where he sat.

"Not that I recall," Blake crooned, way too amused for my liking.

"Smart ass," I retorted, and had been about to bend to retrieve my bag when he rose from the chair. He cleared the space between us in a fraction of a second. And then he was towering over me, his eyes blazing down into my soul.

His hand came around my jaw, rough, and yet soft.

ELENA LAWSON

Vying for dominance but allowing room for me to deny him. His thumb brushed along my chin as he leaned in. His lips were only a breath away from mine as he whispered, "The things I'd like to do to that *smart mouth* of yours."

I shivered, my body responding to him before my mind could catch up. My back arching and chin tipping up, trying to reach him. To taste him.

Fuck. This felt right. It was *right*, wasn't it?

And I mean, if they were intimate with each other, why couldn't I be intimate with all of them, too? Right?

Right. The little minx in the back of my mind nodded vehemently, spreading her legs wide as she hooked a finger in the direction of Blake. *Come to mama,* she growled.

"Do you trust me?" Blake spoke against my mouth, the barest brush of our lips made me shudder, a small sound escaping my mouth.

I looked up into his eyes. Steady. Dark. Aged ten years, but still the boy I fell in love with almost fifteen years ago. "Yes."

He drew something out of his pocket and snapped it the air—the sound loud and sharp, like a whip. My heartbeat spurred into a gallop, leaping into my throat. *Nervous* didn't begin to cover what I was feeling.

Aroused. Apprehensive. Afraid.

The feelings danced and twirled behind my breastbone in a dizzying tango. I could handle pain—that, I knew. And I *did* trust Blake. Vampire or not.

So, what was there to be afraid of?

"Yes," I repeated, nodding this time, my voice more certain. A certainty I think Blake had been waiting to hear in my tone. "Yes, I trust you."

Blake released my jaw in favor of my wrists, he drew them up sharply, pulling them together until he'd coaxed my fingers to clasp one another, palms flush. Then he passed a small length of black silk over my knuckles, the smooth fabric making my skin tingle.

I opened my mouth to ask him what he was doing, but he hushed me before I could speak. "Don't speak," he ordered me.

I bit my lower lip to keep from talking.

Blake peered at me from the corner of his eye as he knotted the fabric and pulled it tight over my wrists. I gasped. "You're still healing," he said. "So, I'll be gentle."

I wasn't about to argue, the nervous fluttering in my belly made it feel like I'd just gone over the edge of a steep hill on a rollercoaster that had no off switch. Exhilarating—but also terrifying.

Since it seemed I wasn't allowed to speak, I nodded instead, gulping.

Blake pulled a second piece of fabric out of his other pocket. This one reminiscent of a silk tie, and I wondered if he'd been wearing it with that fancy suit jacket he had on. And then I wondered why he was wearing a suit jacket at all. Not that I was complaining —he looked damn good in it, and…okay. I needed to shut off my brain. The slumbering dragon in my belly was yawning awake, and the sexy little minx in my mind purred, readying her claws.

Oh god.

I shook as Blake moved into place behind me, trailing a finger over the top of my chest as he went, just above where the towel still covered my breasts. But it was starting to slip—another moment or two and it would be a puddle of plush white around my ankles.

Blake's hands came around either side of my neck and with a snap of the silken tie I was blinded. He secured the tie over my eyes with a knot at the back of my head—pulled tight over my still-damp hair. I could see a small bit of light around the edges, but nothing more. It was pitch dark. I tried to move my hands but the way he tied them together made it near impossible.

I thought if I pulled hard enough, I would be strong enough to unbind myself, but I wasn't certain, and the uncertainly made my pulse quicken and my lips part to lose an alternatingly panicked and lustful breath.

He was so close I could feel his body heat. Smell his clean linen and suede scent—the hints of vanilla soothing my senses—lulling me into a state of temporary calm.

Blake's fingertips grazed my collarbone and I bucked under the soft whisper of his touch. The phantom fingers trailed up my neck, tipping my head to one side with practiced restraint.

Oh fuck.

Fuck.

He was going to bite me.

My toes curled and my stomach flipped. Gooseflesh rose on my arms and legs. The sensation racing over me like a rogue shock wave, igniting all my nerve endings, setting my skin ablaze. The anticipation made every muscle in my body tense, begging to be unwound by the release I would only receive from the piercing of his teeth.

Please. The irrational part of me pleaded. *Please.*

I sensed more than felt him lean in and I jolted as his warm breath caressed the tender spot at the base of my neck, just below my right ear. Blake pressed his lips to my skin, kissing me softly. I could feel the press of his fangs through his lips. I let out a weak moan, wanting so badly to touch him. To see him.

When his lips came away from my skin, I couldn't help it. "Please," I whispered and his hands on my neck stiffened for a fraction of an instant.

"You're still healing," he replied after an eternity of waiting, his words strained. I knew he wanted what I offered—likely more than I, myself, wanted it.

I shook my head. I was feeling *much* better. Maybe not one hundred percent, but close enough. "No… *Please….*"

I licked my lips when his hands tightened on my neck, shivering with pleasure.

"Are you certain?"

I nodded vehemently, feeling a little dirty. Like a druggie who wanted their fix. Except these were my boys. And I was willing to bet it only felt as incredible as it did because of that fact. Sure, there may be some of the same feelings with any vampire who bit me, but the feeling had to be as strong as it was because it was *them.* And to me, that made it the rightest thing in the world.

A sound like a click and a small groan preceded the sound of heavy steps as someone entered the room. I knew those steps. I'd all but memorized the sound in over the last few days. Just like I'd memorized every inch of him whenever I had to chance to stare. Afraid he would vanish again. That being with him again wouldn't last.

Frost stopped walking, and I wanted to turn around and see him, but the blindfold was still secure across my eyes, and Blake's hands were still tight on my neck, holding me in place.

"Couldn't wait, could you?" Frost's gruff voice slithered into the room, making my skin bristle.

Blake didn't answer him.

I was too dizzy with desire to do much more than stand there, my body a live-wire shooting bolts of electricity into my blood—convulsing in shudders and shivers all over the surface of my skin.

"She's still healing," Frost added, mimicking what Blake said only a moment before. "We shouldn't take any of her blood until she's—"

"I know," Blake interrupted him, and I couldn't help the frown that pulled down at the corners of my lips, though…the way Frost said *we* as though he intended to *join* Blake made the lustful little minx in my mind sit up and take notice—near salivating.

I'd never been with two men at the same time before. My knees knocked together and a silky wetness spread between my thighs. What were these guys doing to me?

Fuck.

I wanted them so bad. I tried to pull at my wrists again, wanting to break free, but also so incredibly turned on at the fact that I couldn't. It added another level. Another dimension of pleasure I'd never experienced before. One I wanted to see through until the end.

"I want you," I squeaked, shocked at the high pitch of my voice as I rubbed my legs together, itching for touch. "I want *both* of you. *Now*."

There was a beat of silence before I heard the groan of hinges and the *click* of the door closing firmly in the frame. I grinned, biting my lower lip.

"Take mine," Frost said, and my brows furrowed

until I realized what he meant with a start—truly wanting the blindfold off now. "It will sate you well enough to control the urge to take hers."

So not fair!

I wanted to whine, to stomp my little feet and shout *No! Bite me! I want to be the one to be bitten!*

But Blake was going to feed from Frost, and for some unfathomable reason, it made a delicious ache spread through my lower abdomen. Made my toes curl again. I wanted to see them. As though reading my thoughts, Blake lifted me from the floor. I yelped at the suddenness of the movement, trying to find my bearings as he tucked me into his chest and carried me a few steps until I was on the bed, the silken sheets I'd slept in the night before soft against my skin.

I felt him get onto the bed as the mattress beneath us buckled under his weight. Felt the heat of him as he crawled over me, resting one knee on either side of my hips. What was he doing?

Blake yanked my hands up, pulling tightly until I was half sitting—my back against a mound of pillows. He was doing something with the binds on my wrists. Removing them? No. He was tightening them—or maybe… I heard the *shhh* sound of silk pulled fast and tight against metal. The headboard to the bed was wrought iron—a twisting, curling pattern, and reaching my fingers out, I could feel the cool touch of it against them.

The weight of him on the mattress lessened and I found I could no longer move my hands. He'd literally *tied me to the bedpost.*

Good god.

What now?

There was a dull *thud* and I knew poor Mr. Dickins had been knocked to the floor. I had a feeling he wouldn't be getting much use anymore. I smiled at the thought.

Another presence joined us on the bed, and the towel covering me slipped low, uncovering one of my breasts, exposing it to the cool air in the room. The nipple hardened instantly, and a small sigh tumbled from my lips.

Big hands and the intoxicating scents of worn leather, cloves, and tangy aftershave washed over me as Frost leaned in and pinched the edge of the blindfold against the tops of my cheekbones and tugged it down until it fell against my collar. I blinked to readjust to the light, hungry to see what lay before me.

I was not disappointed.

My lips fell apart in awe of the works of art before me. Somehow, they both managed to get undressed. I assumed Frost was undressing while Blake carried me over to the bed and tied me to it, and Blake undressed quickly while Frost gave me back my sight.

I was practically salivating at the scene before me. *Holy motherfucking shit.*

They were godlike. Tightly coiled muscle. Frost—completely hairless. And Blake…Blake had a whisper of chest-hair near the top middle of his chest. I itched to feel it, but soon, my hungry eyes were drawn to *other* parts of him. His obsidian eyes watched me watch him. Dangerous and glinting in the low light.

Tattoos covered his smooth skin, curling in whorls and abstract images up his arms and across the top of his chest—creeping up his neck. Double sleeves and what looked to be an unfinished chest piece. The black ink suited him more than any form of clothing ever could. And below where the tattoo ended on his chest, a long scar—shining silver and pinkish in color marred his otherwise perfectly sculpted torso.

No—*marred* wasn't the right word. The scar left from the first vampire they ever encountered didn't *mar* him. It *defined* him.

I wanted to kiss every inch of it. Like Frost liked to kiss mine when we made love—his silent apology for not being able to prevent it.

My gaze trailed lower to his tapered hips and his perfect Adonis Belt plunging into the V-shape that was like a fucking flashing sign pointing directly as his exquisite cock. He was already hard—though not fully I suspected—even though he was already a good size. Longer than Frost, but not quite as girthy.

I salivated as I glanced between the two of them. Wishing one of them would say something. Or better yet, *do* something. My body itched with the need to be touched and I tugged at my binds again, whimpering.

"Uh-uh," Blake chastised with a wicked glimmer in his black eyes. He moved into position behind where Frost was knelt right in front of me, between my legs. "You'll have your turn," he purred.

Frost's river-green gaze never left mine as Blake's hands trailed up Frost's thick arms, his muscles flexing. His hardened cock twitched.

Blake continued to trail one hand up, while the other moved around to Frost's chest, pulling the large male back further into him in a sort of embrace. He used his other hand to tip Frost's neck to one with a palm placed against Frost's temple.

Frost surrendered to Blake's desire and tilted his head to the side, submitting to the other male fully. *My* Frost. Bad boy Frost who would never submit to another human being on this earth…but who would submit freely only to me—and it seemed to the other guys as well.

A puzzle of four souls, my mind whispered.

It was painfully beautiful and toe-curlingly *hot* to watch as Blake leaned in and loosed a guttural growl an instant before his mouth opened wide, his fangs slid free, and he bit *hard* into the flesh of Frost's neck.

Immediately, Frost was powerless against the tidal wave of pleasure brought on by Blake's bite. I watched his eyes widen and then the lids grow heavy as he lowered them, submitting to his desire. His hands that were fists only a second before, slackened.

The hand Blake had on Frost's chest moved down as he continued to suckle at Frost's neck until it wrapped firmly around his cock. Frost's stomach muscles clenched, and his body responded to the touch in a way that made my heart thunder behind my breastbone and my breaths come rough and ragged.

A burning began low between my legs. A pulsating ache forming there at the intense *need* to join them.

It wouldn't be completely right until *all* of us were together. Until we were *all* one. Where was Ethan? Fuck, I wanted him, too. I wanted us all to find the places where we fit together and then stay there—complete and whole for the first time in our lives.

I watched, enraptured as Blake stroked Frost's satiny length, gripping him hard and then soft and then hard again as his hand moved back and forth, making Frost rock hard. Droplets of blood dribbled down Frost's collarbone and over his chest.

Blake pulled back with a hiss, his fangs retracting. Dazed, with his lids heavy and eyes glassy, Frost leaned forward onto his elbows. For a second I thought he was inviting Blake to enter him from behind and I was shocked at how much the thought of watching them fuck each other excited me. Making me even wetter than I was a moment before.

But instead, Frost tugged me down by my ankle, so

I was more horizontal, his hand reaching up to squeeze my thigh. Going higher up the hollow behind my knee and curling around my thigh. *Sweet mother of god*, I felt like I would explode the moment he touched me.

His hand skirted into the sensitive skin of my upper thigh, into the dip of my groin and around to my belly until he was hovering over me and his hand closed over the towel in a fist as he wrenched it from my body, exposing me to them both.

My body heaved as though I'd been struck. My head tipped back in anticipation. It was agony. The waiting was going to drive me insane.

When I regained my wits, I tipped my head back down to them, licked my lips and swallowed. "If one of you don't fuck me soon, I'm going to rip these binds to shreds."

Blake quirked a brow behind Frost, amused. Frost must've seen me staring at Blake because he obligingly moved out of the way for Blake to move forward between my legs. Frost positioned himself next to my head, and I tugged at the silky cloth keeping my hands tied together. I wanted to touch him so fucking badly. His cock was almost level with my mouth. If he just leaned in a little…

A hot hand came around my calf and I tore my gaze from Frost to see Blake lifting my leg, effectively turning me onto my side so my knees were together, bent, and I was halfway facing Frost. Blake's cock twitched as he moved it slowly, caressing every inch of my legs and ass as he spread his knees, lowering himself so his cock was level with my sex.

Oh god.

Blake licked his lips and moved a hand down to grip himself, planting his other hand on my ass to keep steady as he rubbed his length against me. Moving the tip in flicking motions against my clit. His dark eyes drank in the sight of me as I moaned, my head lolling back to rest against my arm.

He pressed gently against my opening, easing himself inside of me slowly—allowing me to adjust to his length as he pushed deeper into me, his hand on my ass squeezing tight and his jaw clenched tight as he filled me. I bit my lip so hard I tasted blood as he hilted himself inside of me.

"*Fuck,*" he cried in a whisper under his breath as he shuddered, drawing slowly back out only to plunge back inside, harder this time, his body slapping against my backside with the force of the thrust. I gasped, my lips parting, and as I tipped my head back I saw that Frost had moved in a bit closer.

Glancing up at him, I saw that he was busy watching Blake fuck me with an unparalleled hunger in his gaze. But not jealously. He was getting off on it. Waiting patiently for his turn as he continued to stroke my breast. I leaned forward as far as my binds would allow and took his erect cock into my mouth, surprising him.

He shuddered at the contact and his hips bucked, pushing his length further into my mouth. I moaned, licking the sensitive spot around the tip—flicking my tongue back and forth. He cursed under his breath and his hand fisted into my hair.

Blake growled, his grip on me tightening as he drove into me again and again. I moaned around Frost's cock in my mouth, causing him to shudder. My muscles were contracting, burning—*shaking* as my climax lingered—teasing me—just out of reach as Blake ground his hilt against my wet pussy, moving in circular motions, only pulling out a little as he rubbed against me. Stimulating *everything*.

So fucking *agonizingly* slow…

It was pure torture. Beautiful, painful torture.

I tried to move my hips against him, urging him on. Begging him without words as I brought Frost's cock further into my mouth. He'd begun to move, unconsciously matching my rhythm, his fist tightening in my hair until it was near painful.

Blake snaked his hand down and around my thigh, pausing for an instant to lick his fingers before he settled them over my sex and began rubbing my clit as he pumped into me, on the cusp of finding his own release.

Within seconds I couldn't contain it anymore. The

sensations washing over me were threatening to take me over. Swallow me whole. Blake's cock as he fucked me from the side, his length and girth filling me blissfully as he thrust in and in *and in.* His fingers as they methodically rubbed my clit. Frost's fist in my hair and his hot, *hard* cock in my mouth. My hands bound and wrists straining against the soft silk.

It all came to a head, rising and rising until there was nowhere left to go but down. The force of gravity pulled us all over the edge and we plummeted, all taut muscle and sinew. Sweat and blood. I cried out against Frost's cock and he came into my mouth, hot and salty.

Blake's hands stilled on my body as he grunted, emitting a soft cry of his own as he found his release, pouring himself into me at the same time as I came blissfully untethered. The rope snapped, both literally and figuratively at the force of it. The silk shredded and my hands were unbound, sharp fingernails biting down into the tight muscle of Frost's glutes as I drank him down and my heart shattered in my chest. Frost's mammoth cock acted as a gag to stifle the sound of my screams as a wild orgasm tore through me.

We spiraled together in a torrent of hot, heavy breaths, raw animal sounds, straining muscle, and the euphoric ecstasy of our primal release.

17

The bastards made me forget all about my questions that still needed answering, and the full glass of whiskey that still waited for me out in the kitchen. But, I mean, I wasn't exactly complaining...

I hadn't felt what they made me feel as we all found our release together in...well, I hadn't *ever* felt that way if I was being honest with myself. I'd almost had the urge to cry with the force of the raw, unchecked emotions that'd run through me—undoing the knots that'd taken years to form and breaking down the walls I'd formed around my heart and mind. The walls that I erected to fortify myself. To protect myself from hurt—from pain and *loss.*

It was freeing, but it also brought with it the most terrifying feeling. The knowledge that they could break me even more irrevocably than they had the first time we were separated all those years ago.

I took another small swallow of the amber liquid, gripping the glass tightly with both hands as the searing taste of the whiskey burned a path down my throat.

I'd get my answers soon enough.

"We'll be back in an hour," Frost said as he shrugged on his leather jacket and stuffed his feet into his shoes by the door. I didn't miss how his gaze lingered over my curves—still hungry for me in ways I knew I'd always be hungry for him now, too.

Giving him a nod, I rose from the stool and set the glass down on the countertop, adjusting my skirt so it didn't ride so high. Now, clothes seemed optional, and the twisted little minx within kept drawing attention to how *uncomfortable* they were, whispering for me to take them back off. *What do you need them for anyway?*

I strode over to where he was by the door and wrapped my arms around him, reveling in the spicy scent of him. I breathed him in deep and suppressed the urge to shudder, cursing the swelling of my heart as he held me there against him tenderly. "How does Thai sound?"

Blake and Frost offered to go and gas up Betty and Blake's motorcycle and get me some more food. Once that was done it would be time to go. To Baton Rouge.

To…*home*? Well, to their home, but maybe—just maybe —it could be my home, too.

My stomach fluttered.

"Sounds perfect."

"You sure you wouldn't rather come with us?"

I shook my head. Even though both Blake and Frost insisted to give Ethan his space, I'd decided he had enough already. He still hadn't come out of his room, and I was starting to worry. Worry that I'd upset him more than I thought. Or worse, that maybe he didn't want me here after all. Maybe he wanted me to go.

It broke my heart to think that, but I needed to know one way or the other. If I refused to be their vampire bride, did Ethan not want me? Would he not accept me as his human bride instead?

I had to believe he would. But before we climbed into Betty and I let them lead me home, I had to be certain I was welcome—by *all* of them.

"He took it the hardest," Blake said, and I jumped as he approached us. I didn't hear him coming at all. *Fuck*, no one ever snuck up on me and now it'd happened twice in the last few hours. I needed to get my head straight. Get focused. Back in the game.

Soon, we were going to leave, and I had to be prepared. If anyone came to collect the bounty on my head—I had to make sure my boys didn't become collateral damage in the fight. Looking at Blake's dark eyes and Frost's hard green ones, I knew I'd never allow anything to happen to them—not while I drew breath.

"What?" I said, shaking my head and trying to recall what he'd just said.

"Ethan," he said by way of explanation as he pulled his suit jacket off the peg by the door and I stepped out of Frost's arms. "He still hasn't fully accepted all of this —what we *are* now. You thought he was upset because you refused to become our vampire bride," Blake said gruffly, telling me he was still upset by that fact himself, but slowly coming to terms with it. "But really, he was probably upset that we even had to ask you."

"Yeah," Frost said, agreeing. "And your refusal was just adding insult to injury."

"Oh," I said, my brows pulling together.

"Keep your distance," Frost whispered, his gaze flicking towards the hallway. "Ethan doesn't feed often —on blood bags or otherwise. He only really feeds from us."

Were they afraid he would lose control with me?

It seemed strange to me that Ethan would be the one with the least control of the three—him being so analytical and formulaic about everything—he was always the smartest of us. But then again…if he was *fighting* against the very nature of his new being then I supposed all bets were off.

"Alright, I'll be careful," I said and took Blake's hand, squeezing it. His face darkened at the sweet gesture and I let go almost immediately, wondering if maybe he didn't like to be touched? I took a step away, about to say goodbye and go to Ethan when Blake's hand closed around my wrist and tugged, pulling me in for a rough kiss that stole all the breath from my lungs and made my face heat and my legs clench.

When he pulled away, I was stunned and rocked back on my heels, a bit dizzy.

"Back soon," he purred, running the tip of his index finger down my jaw before he grabbed a jealous looking Frost by the bicep and hauled them both out of the condo, sealing the door behind them.

"Lock it!" I heard Frost call back through the heavy metal door before their footsteps faded down the corridor and I heard the *ping* of an elevator being called up.

18

*I*t took me a fair few minutes to work up the courage to go and find Ethan. If it were anyone else—anyone I didn't *care* about—it would have been nothing. But this was Ethan, and I needed him to hear me out, and to hopefully give me the answers I was looking for.

What Blake said gave me hope that maybe I was being overly paranoid and that he would want to have me with them, too. For a fraction of a second I worried about him losing control with me but dismissed that idea right away. Ethan wouldn't hurt me—I was sure of it.

And the other guys wouldn't have left me alone with him if they really thought he was a threat to my safety. Regardless of whether I could take care of myself or not.

I shut up my inner self and lifted my chin. Every-thing would be fine.

The door to the room where Ethan was was the only closed one in the long hall. I stomped to it, my resolve strengthening, but I faltered when I actually got there and was face to face with the thin panel of wood separating us. I lifted my fisted hand to knock, but paused, swallowing hard.

Please, I sent up a silent plea. *Please let me in.*

"You can come in, Rose," the voice said from the other side, catching me off guard. I dropped my hand and inhaled deeply through my nose and pushed the breath out between my lips as I stepped inside the room.

It was dim inside. A lone lamp poured its white light over a desk covered in papers, making the edges of the room seem darker by comparison. A low, modern bed covered in a simple black blanket was pushed against the wall to my left, centered on the wall. The windows were uncovered and open to the warm, fresh breeze of the late summer evening.

And standing like a gargoyle keeping watch over the teeming streets of Atlanta below was Ethan, leaning against the frame of the window at the far right, his hands tucked into the pockets of his pressed trousers.

The soft beige color of the thick knit sweater he wore a contrast to his dark expression. His light brown hair was tousled, hanging low to partially cover his eyes as he finally turned his head to meet my gaze. A muscle in my jaw twitched as I snapped my mouth shut and ground my teeth at the haunting pain I found in his eyes.

I knew that pain. Maybe not in the same way he did, but for years I'd found that *same* darkness in myself when I beheld my reflection in the mirror. It was a hopelessness. A feeling like no matter what you did it wouldn't matter. Because nothing could ever be the same. Nothing could ever be how you wanted it to be.

But I'd found a way out of that darkness, filling the void with training and soon after—with the temporary relief that came every time I ended one of their lives. And now that void filled again, but this time with something less toxic than murder.

If I manage to find a measure of peace in them— maybe Ethan could find a measure of peace in me, too. If he would allow himself.

"Hi," I said lamely, my hands curling into fists.

Ethan smirked. "I've never known you to be awkward, Rose," he said in that calm, Stillwater voice I'd missed for so fucking long. It melted me.

I opened my mouth to respond, but *awkwardly* closed it again. *Damn.* What was wrong with me?

Where Frost and Blake were creatures of passion and primal urges—and always had been for the most part. Ethan was a different sort. He was analytical.

Calm. Collected. Impossibly smart. And the latter was often to his own detriment as it was now.

Being smart is more a curse than a gift—he'd once said to me with that impish grin of his I'd loved and a shrug that told me it was no biggie even though even my fourteen-year-old self knew he was more serious about that statement than he let on.

"Or to beat around the bush," he added when I still didn't say anything.

I stepped further into the room, moving purposefully toward him, glad when he didn't try to move away from me, though the tension between his brows wound tighter. "Look, about earlier," I said, coming to a stop next to him, leaning against the window frame so I was facing him, casting my gaze down into the lights and sounds of the streets twenty stories below, afraid what I might find in his eyes if I looked too long into them. "I didn't mean to—"

"You didn't," he replied in a hard voice, knowing already where I was going with the thought. "You could never."

"Ethan," I began again, wanting to clear the air.

"Look at me, Rose," he urged me, and I felt the brush of his hand against my wrist. Even that miniscule contact sent my blood rushing through my veins. I tried to get control of my emotions, to make the pounding of my heart calm.

When I finally lifted my head, Ethan offered me a

sad sort of smile that almost broke me. "I'm *so* happy you aren't..." he trailed off, the pain back in his tawny brown eyes.

I cocked my head at him. "So happy I'm not...?" I asked him, confused.

His chest expanded as he inhaled deeply, glancing down at himself.

Oh.

"I'm happy you aren't a vampire."

"But," I started, even more confused now. "I thought you wanted me to be your vampire blood mate thing," I asked, and his hand fell from my wrist and he leaned back away from me. "If I was already a vampire, then I'd have said yes," I admitted, knowing that he wouldn't have already deducted that.

I was sure they were all *disappointed* I wasn't changed. It surprised me to hear him say he was *happy* about it.

"I know," Ethan replied, and now it was my turn to want him to look at me. His stare was fixed outside again—his fists in his pockets. "But I wouldn't wish this *existence* on anyone—least of all you."

Now *that* I could understand. I wouldn't wish it on anyone either. And the part of my heart that broke when Frost showed and told me what had become of him and my other boys would *never* heal right. Not ever.

"I realized," Ethan continued, "Right after I saw you

that I could never request of you what we did to ourselves." He ran a shaky hand over his mouth and chin. "And it was like losing you all over again. I was still coming to terms with the fact that you were *here.* I'd just finished holding you in my arms—feeling and hearing your heart pumping the blood through your veins—when I knew it was all over before it could even *begin.*"

He snapped his eyes up and they bore into me, burrowed down deep to grip me somewhere inside I forgot was there. "I knew then that even if you *had* said yes," his voice rose in pitch and he pushed off the wall, standing at his full height, breathing faster. "And for a second—*for a single fucking selfish second I hoped you would*—I *knew* that if you did agree I would *never* have allowed it."

He gripped me by the shoulders, staring down into my eyes, imploring me to understand.

"Rose, I'd give my life to make sure you *never* lose yours."

I didn't realize I was crying until Ethan came back to himself, checked himself, and released me from his grip as he watched a hot tear sear a path down my cheek.

I had been so wrong.

There I was thinking that he was upset with me because I refused to be a vampire—even if it was my guys who were doing the asking—when really he was upset at himself that he'd even asked at all.

"It's not selfish," I whispered as his hands fell from my shoulders and his body slumped. "I understand. I—I once considered it too, you know…" I trailed off, moving back in closer to him to place my hands against his chest. Though he drew breath hard and fast still, there was no pulse beneath the press of my fingers and another tear fell. My chest ached. "Turning myself to avenge my mom."

Ethan was shaking his head. "It's not fair. Mrs. Ward didn't deserve that. *You* didn't deserve that. And when we found out it was all true—that it really was a *vampire* that'd done it—well it seemed only right to put a pause on everyday mortal life and join the fray. To protect those who couldn't protect themselves, but…"

He didn't have to say it. *But he didn't realize it would mean trading in his soul. He didn't realize how hard it would be to control himself—that the monster he let in could take him over.* I wondered for a brief second if like Frost— Ethan had taken life in the beginning, too.

Frost would have a hard-enough time dealing with that, but Ethan? It would absolutely crush him to know that he took the life of a person that could have been a mother, a brother, or a friend. How could he live with that?

"You're right," I said and gazed up into his face. "My mom didn't deserve what she got—but I blame whatever the *fuck* is wrong with us—with our *family* for what happened to her."

Ethan, curious now and with a furrow in his brow that told me he was confused said, "It doesn't make any sense. You shouldn't be able to compel."

I snorted. "You don't think I know that?"

Ethan placed a hand over the hand on his chest, sending a shudder down my spine. But then he removed it and placed it back down at my side. I bit the inside of my cheek.

"When Frost told us you were human, but that you were strong and you healed fast we had to assume you weren't fully human, either. But none of us really knew what to make of that. You could've been Fae, I suppose? But I doubted that. And you couldn't have been a shifter. I was pretty sure you weren't a witch, either. But then Frost said you could compel..."

He cocked his head at me, his soft brown hair falling to one side to stroke the corner of his eye. *Fuck* he was handsome. Even ten years later, he still had that boyish charm. The soft eyes. The dimples that you could still faintly see even when he wasn't smiling. "It isn't possible," Ethan said, and I saw his jaw clench. He raked a hand down his chin again.

"And yet here I am," I said, spreading my arms wide at my sides with a sigh.

"And yet here you are."

"I know it shouldn't be possible for a human—"

"It's not just that," Ethan said, interrupting me with a dangerous look. "The power to compel lies only with *male* vampires. It's been like that since the dawn of time. Since before the curse of Andora made us unable to walk in sunlight—made us bloodthirsty immortals," he said, and I watched as his eyes widened and then narrowed as he figured something out in his head. I was glad he knew what the fuck he was talking about because he'd completely lost me.

"Since vampires were just Vocari," he finished, searching in my eyes for something as though he could see the answer to a question he had written in the fine print of my stare.

"Ethan, I have no idea what you're trying to tell me right now."

He blinked and swallowed, rocking back on his heels. "It's nothing," he said dismissively. "It's not possible, I just thought…never mind."

"*Ok*," I said drawing out the word.

"We'll figure this out, Rose," he said reassuringly and lifted his hand as though he intended to comfort me, but then dropped it again.

With a deep sigh I stepped away from the wall, drawn to the desk covered in papers and ink drawings against the opposite wall. It was clear Ethan was going to be a tougher nut to crack than the other guys had been. I could tell he wanted to be close with me, but he was afraid.

Whether he was afraid he'd hurt me, or afraid to be hurt if I decided to leave after all, I wasn't sure. Maybe a combination of both. The latter I could understand. But I saw the strength in his eyes that made me know that the former wasn't possible. He'd die before he laid a violent finger on me, or anyone for that matter.

I had to be patient. He was going to need more time.

"Did you draw these?" I asked, lifting the first sketch that caught my eye. It was a stake with a blood-coated tip, hovering amid coiling vines covered in sharp thorns. Another depicted a vampire with pain-filled eyes and a hissing mouth, his hands clutching at the same thorny vines as they choked him, drawing blood from the skin on his neck. Gruesome. And yet beautiful.

Ethan didn't move from the window. "Yeah," he said quietly, and I could *hear* the flush I knew would be staining the tips of his ears pink in his voice.

I noticed the tattoo gun in an open case at the side of the desk and connected the dots. "All of Blake's ink?" I asked. "You're a tattoo artist?" I asked, trying to picture my Ethan in that role.

I'd always thought he would be a scientist, or maybe a professor at a fancy university. Or maybe an archeologist or an engineer. I'd almost forgotten about his love for art. It was often overshadowed by his academic achievements. But he always carried a sketchbook with him back in school. Would never show me what was inside of it, though.

The drawings were incredible. So detailed and intricate. There was something morbid about each one, but that only served to make them even more beautiful. Haunting.

I could see the small smirk on the corner of Ethan's mouth as he turned to me just enough for me to see the small glimmer of pride in his eyes. "I am. Have my own shop and everything—it was the only profession that would allow me to cater to a strictly vampire clientele and still make decent money," he explained.

Of course, he would be the one to still at least attempt a normal life. "It's called Moonlit Ink," he told me. "And it's the only one of its kind. Tattoos generally don't *stick*," he said, using air-quotes to emphasize his point, "to vampires. Our flesh heals too fast for the ink to settle, and even then, sometimes our bodies reject it, just like they reject metal, or any sort of surgical implants."

I hadn't known that.

"But, with my formula—they stick."

Immortal tattoos, pretty fucking badass if you asked me.

"Can I have one? A tattoo, I mean?"

Ethan seemed taken aback by the question and it took him a moment to consider it. "Maybe," he said honestly. "Your blood—humans bleed when they get tattooed. It's why I only cater to vampires."

"I trust you."

His gaze darkened and he looked away. "You shouldn't."

"Don't do that, Ethan," I told him, getting fed up with all the brooding and self-loathing business. I moved back to where he stood sentinel by the window and poked him in the chest. "You're the best of us, you know. And I don't care what you think, I *know* you're still you in there. Just like Frost is still Frost and Blake is still Blake. Fuck, if anyone isn't who they once were anymore, it's *me!*"

I shocked myself with the statement, realizing how true it was. Frost may have killed a few people, maybe Blake and Ethan had, too, but I'd killed *hundreds* of vampires.

And if even a fraction of them had been like my guys—living by a code—not taking human lives, then *I* was the monster, wasn't I?

The guilt settled in my stomach like a pool of lead before I drew in a shaking breath and shoved the feeling away. I couldn't deal with those thoughts right now—not with everything else going on. And besides —the majority of the vampires I'd killed attacked *me* first.

Don't think about it.

I'd gotten real good at dismissing painful thoughts

since mom. I could shove them so deep down that they all but vanished into the chasm I kept hidden in my heart.

It was then I realized that Ethan needed me. He needed someone to tell him he wasn't a soulless monster—to remind him when he forgot. And maybe to help him through this new life he asked for but didn't understand the consequences of. "I'm coming with you guys to Baton Rouge whether you like it or not," I told him. "You're fucking stuck with me."

His eyes lit up and his lips parted—his body went rigid with shock, and even beneath the knit sweater, I saw how muscular he was. Leaner than Blake and Frost, but I'd wager almost just as strong. His muscle was lean and coiled, like a deadly snake ready to strike.

"I'm serious," I went to continue when he just kept standing there stoic with that adorable dumbfounded expression on his face. "I—"

He crushed me into his arms. This wasn't the soft, gentle hug he gave me when I first came out of the room earlier. It wasn't hesitant. He wasn't trying to gauge my reaction and act accordingly. This was a *fucking bear hug* that threatened to squish all the air from my lungs. But I didn't care. I wrapped my arms around him, too, as tightly as I could. Who needed to breathe anyway, right?

I buried my face in his knit sweater, thinking I wouldn't ever be able to get enough of that smell. The smooth nautical scent of his cologne, like ocean spray mixed with the sweet musk of the natural smell that was just *Ethan*.

"I didn't think you would—" Ethan said, stopping himself mid-sentence.

I pulled away so he could see into my eyes. "Did you really think I was going to leave you? That I would *ever* allow you to leave me ever again?"

Ethan smiled. A huge face-splitting smile that filled the universe and stroked the dark places inside of me with light. I swatted him on the arm playfully. "As if you actually thought you were going to get rid of me that—"

He kissed me. His pillow-soft lips came down on mine swiftly, but with a gentleness that made me gasp and moan all at the same time. The tenderness of it threatened to shatter me—to break through what little of my walls remained in place over my heart. It was a cloud of butterflies raining down into my stomach and a warm ache spreading out to my limbs.

His right hand cupped the back of my head while his left pressed me firmly against him with a flattened palm on my lower back. Our breaths mingled, hot and heavy as the kiss deepened, spurred on by my hands as they grabbed fistfuls of his hair, wanting to draw him even nearer.

I shivered as his fangs came out, the hard teeth pressing against my lips. That same dangerous longing for the venom of the bite had me feverish—near quivering. My desire-addled brain taking over.

Ethan's mouth moved from my lips to kiss the corner of my mouth, and then my cheek—the spot below my ear. My breath hitched and he growled, tearing himself away from me with a guttural snarl. He was across the room in the blink of an eye, his body *slammed* against the wall, his breaths coming hard and ragged as he held himself there with fingers *literally* dug into the drywall.

A loud *bang* outside the room sent me spinning into motion. That sixth sense I'd developed over the years made my hair stand on end. Footsteps in the entryway —stomping down the hall. I drew my stakes.

Ethan gave a quick *what the fuck?* look as I pulled them out from their holsters beneath my skirt and then assumed a fighting stance at my side, his fangs bared for an entirely different reason now.

The door flew open, nearly blown from its hinges as Frost came barreling through, his expression hard with the sharp glint of panic. Blake wasn't far behind him and his handsome face screwed up at the sight of Ethan and I on the balls of our feet, having almost attacked them.

"Well at least you're dressed," Blake breathed, stomping back out of the room with purposeful strides.

"We need to leave...*now*," Frost said through gritted teeth. "Get your shit. We don't have long."

Ethan and I shared a look as Frost turned from the room. Ethan set to gathering up his things—shoving them into a small duffel, while I followed Frost out right on his heels. "What is it? What's going on?" I asked, my hands tightening on the metal stakes in my fists, my blood chilling.

Frost didn't stop to chat, speaking as he moved through the condo, grabbing a small bag from just inside one of the rooms, as though he'd been expecting this and was already all packed up to go. "They know you're here," he said gruffly, tossing the bag onto his shoulder. "They're *fucking everywhere.*"

What?

"But, how? We didn—"

"I don't know," he hissed, shoving my duffel bag into my arms as we entered my room, the still rumpled sheets on the bed smelled of us, but now they were cold and empty. The emotions they held atop them soured and grown cold in the face of what was happening now. "But the whole goddamned city is crawling with them. Maybe they found the one you killed? Or maybe —*hell*, I don't fucking know Rosie—maybe he hadn't been alone? Maybe one followed us here and I," he seethed, clenching his fists. "I was so worried about you that I didn't notice…"

He was throwing clothes into the duffel—he even tossed Mr. Dickins at me and I tucked him into the opening. "Are you sure?"

He nodded once, tight.

It was less than a week ago that I even *found out* about the price on my head. And now there were enough of them here—after me—that Frost was this worried? It was rare to see anything even remotely close to *fear* in his eyes, but that's exactly what I saw now.

If it was enough to make Frost afraid—then I figured I should take it seriously. I steeled myself and bent to stuff everything in my bag and zip it up. "Alright. What's the plan?"

"We leave here. Head to Baton Rouge. Make sure we aren't followed. We can hole up there until we come up with a plan."

There was just one thing about this plan that I didn't agree with... as long as they were with me, they were going to be targets, too. They would be in danger. And strong or not, they were still too young to stand their ground against a massive group of vamps that could be *hundreds* of years older.

I'm the one who made a name for myself with my blood-thirsty trade. I'm the one they want. Not them.

Not my boys.

"No. We need to separate. I'll head south. You guys head home. I'll come to you there when it's safe to."

He looked at me like I was insane. "That's not happening Rosie," he growled. "You're staying with us. How else are we supposed to make sure noth—"

"*I can take care of myself,*" I hissed, hefting my duffle onto my shoulder. *Fuck,* why did he have to insist on trying to protect me. *They* were the ones who needed protecting, couldn't he see that? They were no more than puppies staring down a pack of rabid wolves.

"Hey," Frost barked, gripping me by the shoulder to stop me from walking out the door.

I hit his arm away with my forearm. "*Don't.*"

"Stubborn as a goddamned *mule!*" he all but shouted. "Listen here, woman. You are *stuck with us.* Fucking *deal with it.*"

The fucking brute!

"The hell I am!"

When I turned again, I found a wall of muscle in my path. Both Blake and Ethan were in the doorway, blocking my exit. Both had their shoes on and were carrying their bags. Blake had traded in his tailored suit jacket for a thick leather one that accentuated his broad shoulders. A motorcycle helmet hung off the strap of his satchel. He held a length of rope in one fist and was looking at me with a challenge in his gaze.

Ethan looked apologetic, but by his stance, I knew he wouldn't be budged, either.

Motherfuckers.

"Whether you come willingly or not is up to you, luv," Blake purred, drawing out a length of rope between his hands and snapping it tight.

Rage made my hands shake and pulse quicken, but

it was already evaporating. The red tinge in my vision fading.

"We're stronger as one," Ethan added reason to Blake's brutish threat. "Please don't make us force you."

"You're insane. All of you are *fucking insane.*"

None of them moved. None answered me.

I closed my eyes and calmed myself—taking a moment to soothe the riotous surge of adrenaline. Ok. It wasn't as though I was going to barrel through them. And for all we knew the vampires who were after me didn't even know what I looked like. Maybe this wasn't so bad. It would be alright, right?

I huffed, opening my eyes. "*Fine*. I'll go with you."

Ethan sighed. Blake tucked the length of rope back into his bag, and I flinched as Frost placed a hand on my shoulder. "Ethan's right you know—we're stronger together. Always have been."

With my heart in a vise, I turned to meet his gaze over my shoulder. Furious and terrified, but also relieved in a way—though I couldn't have explained why. "We go quietly," I said in a low, cutting voice. "Straight to the truck, and then straight to the highway. We don't stop until sunrise."

"Agreed."

I glanced at the clock beside the bed. We had a little over four hours until we'd need to stop.

With any luck—they'd never know we left.

he condo building outside the door to the unit the guys rented was quiet as we exited. Thank fuck because no matter how many times the guys asked me, I refused to put away my stakes. If anyone saw us, I'd just compel them to *unsee* us.

Besides, with the guys surrounding me in a spearhead formation—Frost at the head, Ethan to my left, and Blake to my right—no one would even be able to *see* me, much less notice what I was carrying in my hands.

I wasn't exactly chill with this set-up, but I figured it would be easier to allow them to do what came naturally, even if their worries were unfounded. I could vault over Frost in half a second if I needed to, so it really didn't matter much who walked where.

As another condo owner came off the elevators and

passed us in the hallway, I had my feelers out for that *otherness* that would tell me if they were a vampire or not. I didn't feel anything, but with a wall of the creatures I hunted all around me, interrupting the flow of energy, I couldn't be certain. The startled older gentleman let out a little yip as we passed by him as he hurriedly tried to insert his slim silver key in the lock of his unit.

Though humans didn't have the same sense I did, there was a natural *bad feeling* associated with vampire-kind for them. Sort of like when you met someone you knew right off was just *bad* or *trouble*. Animals sensed it much easier.

Frost jammed the arrow for down and it lit up, the doors *pinging* open for us almost instantly. Figures there wouldn't be too many people calling it in the middle of the night on a weekday.

Frost entered and Blake ushered me inside with them. I grit my teeth. I fucking *hated* elevators. How often did the metal cords holding them elevated snap? I shuddered.

"You alright?" Ethan asked in a whisper-soft voice, an apology laced the words. He obviously didn't relish the fact that they basically gave me no other choice than to go with them. Unlike Blake, who seemed almost smug when I submitted to their demands. I was going to punish him for that. Sadistic fucker.

And yet…I couldn't help admiring the curve of his glutes as the elevator dropped.

"Rose?" Ethan again.

I cleared my throat. "Oh. I'm fine," I said. "Just hate elevators."

No one else said a word until we were stepping out into the parking garage below the building. The bright white lighting seared my eyes, and the familiar smell of oil, exhaust and rubber filled my nostrils. I'd slept in so many parking garages over the years, I'd come to truly love that smell. Drawing in a deep breath, I found it brought me a modicum of comfort.

And if that didn't help soothe my excited nerves, the sight of Black Betty—shiny from a fresh waxing by the look of it—did the rest. And beside her lounged a matte and shiny silver metal beast of a bike. A Ducati Diavel if I wasn't mistaken. The very same bike I almost bought myself with my inheritance instead of Betty. But Betty had the trunk-space for a body—the Diavel did not.

I felt a little lighter knowing that all we had to do now was get on the road. They shouldn't have any idea what Betty looks like and once we were out of Atlanta —they'd lose us for sure.

Almost home free.

We'd figure out what to do about the little problem I'd created for myself when we got there. I had a feeling there may need to be a lull in business for the Black

Rose—the guys would want me to lie low—probably stop killing—and *definitely* stop leaving roses altogether —for the foreseeable future. Would they still help me bring vengeance to the ones who deserved it, though? Would they help me find the bloodsucking fucker who killed my mother? I hoped so.

But we'd sort it all out once I knew they were hidden away safe.

"Of course, you have that fucking bike," I said under my breath, more to myself than to anyone else, really.

Blake chuckled and dangled the keys in front of me. "If you behave yourself maybe I'll take you for a ride sometime, hmm?"

"Ha!" I snipped, snatching the keys from his grasp faster than he could blink. "How about I take *you* for a ride?"

Blake narrowed his black eyes at me, zeroing in on the keys I now dangled in front of *his* face.

Frost stepped up behind me. "It's a good idea actually—Rose drives like a bat out of hell—if any vamps are paying any attention whatsoever to the roads, she'll draw suspicion in the truck."

Before I realized what he was doing, he'd wrested the keys from my grasp and tossed them back to a snickering Blake. "You drive, though," Frost said. "And no fucking around on that thing until we're far from here, got it?"

I rolled my eyes at Frost and resisted the urge to

stick my tongue out at Blake, who looked far too pleased with himself for my liking. "It's going to take *ages* to get to Baton Rouge with you lot driving," I groaned, throwing my hands up. "Which one of you is going to drive Betty, then?"

I looked between Frost and Ethan, my hands on my hips.

"Betty?" Ethan asked, lifting a brow.

"Her truck. She named it."

Ethan glanced at my baby and nodded. "Black Betty. Original."

"Oh, shut up," I said, and tossed Ethan the keys to my truck. He caught them midair. "You drive her—I trust you to take better care of her than this brute." I jerked my head toward Frost and hefted my duffel bag at him. He caught it with an *oomf* and shook his head.

"You've driven that hunk of metal into the ground yourself, Rosie. Don't think there's much more damage we could do," Frost said, his words trailing in his wake as he and Ethan wove through the parking garage to where Betty waited.

Dick.

"You still good with cars?" I asked Blake, turning back to face him, suddenly exhausted and eager to get moving.

He nodded. "Last I checked."

"Good."

He lifted a brow but said nothing. Likely Blake

would just tell me to buy a new one—that Betty was on her last leg, but I was certain there were ways I could bribe him to fix her up for me.

"Shall we?" I said, gesturing to the bike.

Blake removed the matte black helmet from the strap on his bag and passed it to me. "You really shouldn't be riding in a skirt," he said, his eyes drawing a sizzling line down my legs to the combat boots strapped to my feet.

I took the proffered helmet and sighed. "Just don't crash, mmkay?"

Blake's jaw clenched. "Get on," he growled.

Yes, sir!

I had to adjust the straps a bit but managed to get the helmet to fit snugly enough on my head. Then I climbed onto the seat behind Blake as he started the engine. My hands came around Blake's middle and he flinched. When I breathed against the back of his neck, his hair rose, and his body shuddered.

"Visor down," he commanded, and I did as I was told, swiping down the veil of hard plastic.

We watched Betty pull out of the parking garage and Blake revved the engine. The vibrating roar settled into a rich purr as we followed them out into the night.

GETTING out of the north end of downtown was a nightmare. It was a damn good thing I wasn't driving because I'd have pulled some highly illegal shit to get us out of the thick, honking, blinking traffic and onto the I-85. I felt like we were all sitting ducks in the tightly packed streets.

I could have sworn I felt the presence of other vampires near us, but it was hard to tell the difference between them and my guys. I couldn't be sure. Either way, I would be happy once we were away from this place and out onto the open highway—though that brought with it its own troubles.

At least here there were bystanders—thicker than the teeth in a comb. And traffic cameras. Most vamps wouldn't be stupid enough to try to attack us in full view of the public eye. There were laws about that sort of thing. The oldest of the vampires dealt with the ones who broke those laws. From what I knew there was a sort of hierarchy. A matriarchy if I wasn't mistaken— with the head honcho of the lecherous race the eldest changed female vampire known to the world.

All I knew was that whoever Queen Bitch was, she must have some serious pussy game to control that many vampires…since apparently, she couldn't even compel.

There was a break in the traffic up ahead and within a few more minutes we were moving again—at a pace that had me grinding my teeth—but moving, nonetheless. We watched Ethan turn Betty onto a side street ahead of us and followed. What were they doing?

We were supposed to head straight for the I-85 and out of the city.

I felt a vibration in the chest area of Blake's leather jacket and faintly heard a cellphone ringing. He was still driving, so I unzipped it and reached my hand inside to dig around for the phone. It was warm against his chest, and I had to bite my bottom lip to stop myself from exploring *other* areas beneath his clothes.

Clearing my throat, my hand closed around the cell in his slim pocket and I pulled it out and saw the caller ID said *Frost*. I hit the green button and slid the cell under the base of the helmet so I could hear him.

"Hey," I said before he could speak. "Why did you get off the main road?"

"It's on the radio," he replied. "An accident up on I-85—that's why the traffic is so bad right now. We'll take the I-20 instead."

I didn't know this area all that well, but I didn't like the look of the route we were taking. There was hardly anyone else on the road, or the sidewalks. I mean, I didn't expect there would be at one in the morning, but we were meant to stick to the main streets and get straight onto the highway from down-town. "Alright," I said hesitantly. "Just hurry it up, will you?"

"Will do," he replied in his gruff voice before the line went dead. I put the cell back where it was and zipped up Blake's jacket. Opening the visor of my helmet a bit, I shouted to Blake, "There's an accident. We're taking the I-20 instead."

He nodded that he heard and sped up, matching Betty's new, quicker pace as we maneuvered through the side-streets on a roundabout path to get to the other way out of the city.

We turned down a one-way and up ahead, past Betty's big black ass, I could see the shine of headlights on what looked to be the street that would take us to the exit ramp. I blew out a breath. The buzzing in my blood that had begun earlier was quickening again. Even though there was barely a breeze and the night was warm, the tiny hairs on my thighs stood on end. My skin bristled.

Shit. There was a vampire. And not one of the three that were with me. This one was fucking *old.* I craned my head all around, trying to spot him. Trying to see if he'd spotted *us.* But the fucking helmet made it near impossible to see anything more than what was right in front of me.

"What is it?" I heard Blake call back to me and I reached down between my legs to draw out a stake.

I undid the clip and wrenched the helmet off. "We've got company," I said in a low voice, knowing he would hear, and hoping my voice was low enough that wherever the vamp was, he *couldn't.* "We need to get off this street."

The one-way was vacant save for the truck and

Blake's bike. Tall brick walls closed in on us from either side. Nothing more than fire-escape ladders clung to the sides. Closed, curtained windows and the electric humming of air conditioners dotted the identical apartment buildings all the way up to the top. No sign of the vamp.

Blake flashed his headlight at Betty and revved the engine again. "Hold on," he called back to me and kicked the Diavel into a higher gear. We sped passed Betty, closing the distance between us and the open mouth of the exit.

I fumbled and dropped the helmet, leaning forward and tightening my thighs on either side of the seat to keep from falling off. I held the stake down at my side with a vise-like grip and peered back at Betty. I could just make out the shadows of Ethan and Blake in the cab as they too began to speed up.

I whipped my head around, finding we had only another block or two to cover. When I looked back, my stomach pooled with dread and my body came alive with the spark of adrenaline. A lit match to the gasoline in my veins.

A third shadow had joined the other two. Except this one wasn't in the cab—this one was standing on the road in front of them. The headlight obscured any detail I may have been able to pick out about him. The shadow was tall and thick. In a braced stance with its arm bent as though about to swing.

My mouth fell open in a high-pitched gasp. I'd meant to shout. To scream. To tell them to stop—but it all happened so fast. One second Betty was barreling down the one-way street headlong after us. And the next my ears were filled with the sickening sounds of screeching tires, broken glass, and the deafening crunch and groan of metal as the truck wrapped around the immovable object planted in its path.

"Stop!" I shouted, finally finding my voice, but Blake only roared. A guttural, pained sound that flowed into my ears like poison and tainted me on the inside—making my heart pound harder against my ribcage.

He didn't stop.

I flung myself from the still-moving bike, tucking my body into a roll. I hit the damp asphalt with a scraping *thunk* and rolled, pain exploding into my knees, my arms, and all up my side. Finding my footing after rolling half the distance, I swayed a bit before the double vision settled and drew my other stake.

Betty was a gnarled mess in the road. Her hood was concave, as though they'd wrapped her around a pole instead of a creature made from the same substance as me. Smoke wafted up from the hood in plumes and tendrils, filling the air and my nose with the reek of hot metal and engine grease. *Fuck.* I couldn't see through it to see if Ethan and Frost were alright.

And the vampire was gone.

"Frost?" I shouted, hearing the screech of braking

tires as Blake pulled around to turn back, shouting something I couldn't hear. "Ethan?"

"They're dead."

I whirled around and raised my stakes, ready to impale the *fuck* out of the bastard, but he was quicker. He was *so much quicker* I couldn't even fathom the movements he made. Hands came around my face—covering it with something soft and wet.

A sweetness wet my lips and I pulled in a hard breath. The ether-like smell clogged my nostrils and numbed my throat. I tried to fight him—I scratched and pounded on the arms holding me, but it was like clawing at solid steel. Even when the wetness of his blood started running down my hands, he didn't so much as flinch.

The double vision returned as I whimpered into the chloroform-soaked cloth and had to watch, helpless as twin Blake's leapt from their motorcycles, murderous intent in their glittering eyes—fangs bared. I had no doubt Blake would have fought with everything he had to get me out from the clutches of the creature that'd captured me…had it not been for the shadow that swooped down from above, dual blades drawn as it rammed him into the wall.

No.

I couldn't see him anymore. And the sounds of the street were growing distant, garbled. A lone tear streaked down my face. Somewhere behind us a horn honked. And somewhere in the blinding light of the intersecting street ahead, a woman was screaming.

My body weakened, and even though I was screaming inside. Cursing and seething and *aching.* I could do nothing as my body gave in to the chemical and sagged against the ancient vampire behind me. My arms fell limp against my sides and my head lolled back, eyelids fluttering closed.

"That's it," the vampire crooned. "It will all be over soon."

here the ever-loving fuck am I?

I awoke in stages. First a twitch of my fingers. Then the scrape of my bare legs against something soft—like animal fur. Blinking away a sticky residue, I tried to take in my surroundings, but the dizziness made me immediately shut my eyes again. My stomach lurched and I found the strength to move just enough to vomit over the side of whatever weird fuzzy *thing* I'd been laid out on.

Once my stomach was finished heaving, I dragged a leaden arm across my mouth, wiping away the disgust from my lips. My lungs seared with each breath, and there was an uncomfortable feeling in my nose like someone had stuffed wads of tissue up there. But when I prodded the area with my fingers, there wasn't anything there.

What happened?

Why couldn't I remember what—

It came back in broken pieces. Holding tight to Blake as his Diavel roared down the one-way street. Betty's headlights right before she crashed into a pillar of ancient flesh. My back against a stranger as he held me with an iron grip—smothering me with a chloroform-soaked cloth.

"Fuck," I cursed, trying to move. I *needed* to move. I scanned the room and found it was lit only a roaring fire blazing in a hearth of stone. The flickering orange light hurt my eyes and made my head throb. I was on a...bed of some kind. Though in place of blankets there were animal skins covering it in a thick, lush pelt.

What the hell?

I swallowed, wincing as my throat squeezed painfully, dry and feeling as though full of razorblades.

I have to find the guys.

I had to make sure they were alright. That they weren't here.

Maybe the other vampires had left them alone. It was me they wanted, right?

And then I remembered the words of the vampire as he whispered into my ear, *they're dead.* My stomach dropped and my heart rose to my throat, choking me as it thudded hard and fast there. No. They could've survived that crash. And Blake...Blake only had one of them to contend with—he could have beat him.

Yes.

They're ok.

They're ok.

It was what I needed to tell myself to be able to keep moving. To do what I needed to do to get out of this godforsaken place and find them. I reached between my legs and left around the leather straps there but came up empty. My stakes were gone.

I had to stifle a scream as I lifted my body from the bed—the sound coming out like a hiss instead. Something in my foot had broken and it hadn't set right as it healed.

Pain shot up through my calf and I had to bite down hard to stop the sounds from escaping my lips, my eyes watering with the effort of containing it.

Gripping one of the tall wooden bedposts I hobbled over to the fireplace and reached out for the metal poker with shaking fingers. It felt so heavy. Like a bowling ball instead of a thin stick of metal with a pointed end.

I had the distinct feeling I'd been out longer than I thought. Chloroform shouldn't have kept me knocked out this long—but who knew how many times they'd held that rag to my face while I was passed out? By the burning in my lungs, I would guess more than once.

The hairs on the back of my neck pricked and my blood chilled.

"About time," the deep voice crooned from the

shadows near what looked to be a doorway at the other end of the space. "You can put that down now," he said, and I could just make out the shape of his arm as he gestured to the poker gripped in my right hand and pointed at the floor. "It really isn't any use to strugg—"

"Where are they?" I snapped, crying out when I tried to move too quickly toward the asshole whose voice, I recognized to be the same as the one who knocked me out. "What have you done with them?"

"Not even a little curious why you're here?"

What?

"I said, *where are they?*"

If he said they were dead, I'd rip his fucking head off.

He crossed his arms and an annoyed *guffaw* sound before he moved like a breeze into the light—almost like he was hovering on air. Not constrained by the laws of gravity.

Who the fuck is this guy?

As the light of the fire fell over his features, I quickly dropped my head. I'd seen enough to know that he was tall—slim but built well. The vampire had a long mane of waving russet brown hair, strong cheek-bones beneath his flawless pale skin and lips any woman would kill for. That was where I'd stopped. If I'd looked into his eyes…I had no doubt he would've had mc bent to his will in an instant.

He was beautiful.

And *terrifying.*

The decay of time held no sway over him. He had to be hundreds of years old but didn't look a day over thirty.

My compulsion would be no match against a vampire as old as I sensed he was. I'd never felt anything like it—this haunting, bone chilling feeling. He must've been older than any I'd ever encountered. The aura of timelessness pulsed off him in bloodcurdling waves.

Again, that voice in my head asked, *who are you?*

"Azrael," he said.

The fuck?

"You curse a lot."

I gasped. He could read my thoughts. *Oh my fucking god he can ready my thoughts.* I shook my head to clear it, staring at his lower legs in horror. *Okay.* Didn't know that was a thing. Apparently, it is. Digest. Get over it. Move on.

The guys. I still needed to know where the guys were. Then I could kill this fucker and be on my—

"Your *guys* are perfectly fine. Out searching for you as we speak, I'm sure."

"But you said—"

"Yes, well I originally thought it would be wiser to kill them, but when you reacted so violently to that idea, I thought perhaps I should leave them alive—I'd rather a cooperative Rose than a feisty one."

Cooperative?

"Yes. Pliant. So long as you do what I ask of you— they will remain alive and safe."

"Get out of my head," I growled, vibrating now. I wanted to lunge at him. To attack. The guys would be going *mental* looking for me if what he said was true. I needed to find them.

"I don't lie."

"Get the fuck out of my head," I said, almost lifting my head, but remembering it was too dangerous to look him in the eye.

How was I supposed to get out of here when this bastard could anticipate my every move? It was hopeless to even try.

"Then you should listen to what I have to say."

I ground my teeth. The violation of knowing someone was rooting around in my mind— tampering with private thoughts and feelings made me see red. *No one* had ever violated me like this. Not ever. And yet I was powerless to stop the invisible assault.

"I'll get out of your head if you put the poker down," he said as though speaking to a child. "And promise to hear me out."

I didn't see that I had much choice. "I'm listening," I said, but my grip only tightened around the metal handle of the poker. There was no way in hell I was going to lower my only weapon. Not a chance.

"Very well," he said, folding his hands neatly behind his back, a note of impatience in his deep baritone. "I've brought you here for a purpose, Rose."

I cringed at the casual use of my name, but more so at how it managed to sound like a caress on his lips— and how it made my mouth go dry.

"May I?" he asked, gesturing to a high-backed leather chair several feet away from where I stood.

I moved back several steps until I was leaning against the bedpost and nodded. He took a seat and I averted my gaze, careful not to allow his eyes to lock onto mine. He moved like water. Pouring himself into the seat like I'd pour whiskey into a rounded glass. I itched to see the expression on his face—to try to discern his motives—what he was thinking.

What he was planning.

But I'd be damned if I let him take control of me. I dropped my head, my eyes trailing along the swirling pattern in the thin rattan carpet.

My pulse quickened. This *thing* before me was the epitome of vampire.

The epitome of a monster.

I wanted nothing more than to end him.

"So much fury in so small a package," he said in a low, rumbling voice, more to himself than to me.

"*Well?*" I snapped. "Start talking."

I was done waiting. Done playing this little game of cat and mouse. He caught me. *Bravo vampire fucker.* Cue applause.

Now good fucking luck holding me if you don't plan to kill me.

"Kill you? Why on earth would I want to kill the last living pure-blooded Vocari?"

"You said you'd get out of my head!" I hissed.

He didn't respond, and it took a moment for what he'd said to register in my head. The last…what?

"Vocari?"

Still, he remained silent. My mind raced. I didn't understand. *Vocari.* I knew that word. It was the ancient term for vampire, wasn't it? Ethan had used the word, too. *Since vampires were just Vocari*—that was what he'd said.

"You didn't know," the vampire called Azrael said, more a question than a statement of fact.

I shook my head. "I'm human."

"Only partly…" he trailed off, drawing in a breath. "I hardly believed it myself when the filthy urchin came to me with what he saw. *A human woman*—he told me, *with eyes like amber who moves like we do…a human woman who can compel a vampire.*"

The one that got away. *Damnit.* I knew that would come back to bite me in the ass and now it had. *Stupid mistake.*

"I'd encountered this phenomenon only once

before, but unfortunately the subject died," the way he said *subject* made me shiver. Was that what I was now? Some sort of subject? To be poked and prodded and studied under bright lights?

"Say you're right—say I *am* this *Vocari* thing. Why does it matter? What is it you want?"

The vampire sighed again—heavily this time. He leaned forward and placed his elbow on his knees. I dropped my gaze lower, but kept my eyes trained on his polished leather shoes, waiting for any sign of movement so I would be ready if he sprang up and tried to attack. "There is so much you don't know," he said. "So much for you to learn..."

With my heart still beating in my throat and an ache forming on the precipice of my skull, I jabbed the poker toward him. "Explain it," I urged him, the stain of weaker emotion discoloring my voice. I needed to know.

Now—faced with the truth of what I was—now more than ever I felt I *needed* to hear it. The reason why I am the way I am. Why my mother and her mother back and back and back had this strange ability.

Why? What was the purpose?

What am I?

"Would it be enough to know that I believe your blood can reverse the effects of the curse?"

My brows drew together and my hand flexed around the handle of the poker at the mention of my blood. Was that what he wanted from me? A drink? "I'm not following."

"Your pure Vocari bloodline might be able to make a vampire able to withstand sunlight—it could make a vampire no longer a slave to thirst," Azrael's tone had changed. As he spoke it became strained and hopeful, filled with longing. "I've seen it once before. I know it's possible. It may even be possible—with enough time and research—to reverse the effects *permanently*."

I've never *felt stronger. I haven't had even a lick of thirst since,* that was what Frost told Blake when I awoke in the condo. Could this *Azrael* person be right?

"I realize you've spent much of your adult life *killing* my kind." You'd think he'd have sounded angry about that tidbit, but he didn't. He stated it as though more impressed than anything. I didn't know what to make of it. "But you also *love* three of them."

My lips parted, but no words came out. I'd been about to deny it but found I couldn't. It was true. I did love them. I'd loved them since I was eleven years old. They were my best friends. And now they were even more than that.

"What if I told you it was possible to *undo* what was done to them?"

My eyes welled and my throat burned. No—it wasn't possible. Once changed, only the true death could end a vampire's immortal life.

"What if I told you it was possible to give them true life again?"

I'd give anything for that. I didn't dare say it aloud, not wanting him to know just how tightly he had me in his grasp with that offer. If it were even remotely possible, how could I not at least try?

What sort of *friend* would I be to them if I didn't?

"All I ask of you is for you to remain under my protection—and for you to offer me your blood when I have need of it. In exchange, I will not harm you or those you love," he paused, and I sensed a change in the air. My heartbeat slowed. "In exchange I can give you what you want most."

My boys. He would give me my guys back. Whole. *Alive.*

My mind was racing, trying to take in everything he was saying. It all seemed so impossible. And *fuck* if it made *any* goddamned sense to me at all, but...

"Do we have an agreement?"

I tossed the metal poker onto the fur-covered bed and lifted my head, meeting the vampire's gaze head-on. A sly grin spread over his features. His high cheek-bones were heavily shadowed in the light of the fire. His lips full and twisted up at one side. The firelight tinted his hair with threads of copper and gold. The skin at the corners of his eyes was crinkled.

And when the log burning in the hearth split—a sizzling *pop* preceding the eruption of sparks from the ashes, the shadows beneath his brows came into startling clarity.

Eyes, bright and piercing, one brown and one blue.

Follow the story of The Black Rose in PROVOKE ME, The Last Vocari, Book 2!
Get it here: mybook.to/provokeme

Printed in Great Britain
by Amazon

19706562R00123